THE EDGE OF IN BETWEEN

Also by Lorelei Savaryn

The Circus of Stolen Dreams

THE
EDGE
OF
IN BETWEEN

LORELEI SAVARYN

VIKING

VIKING

An imprint of Penguin Random House LLC, New York

First published in the United States of America by Viking,
an imprint of Penguin Random House LLC, 2022

Visit us online at penguinrandomhouse.com.

Library of Congress Cataloging-in-Publication Data is available.

Printed in the USA

ISBN 9780593202098

1 3 5 7 9 10 8 6 4 2

LSCH

Edited by Liza Kaplan
Design by Monique Sterling
Text set in Birka LT Pro

For Kayla and her children

THE EDGE OF IN BETWEEN

If you look the right way, you can see that the whole world is a garden.

—The Secret Garden

"What needs could I have," she said, "now that I have all? I am full now, not empty. I am in Love Himself, not lonely. Strong, not weak. You shall be the same. Come and see."

—C. S. Lewis, The Great Divorce

Everyone is born with a measure of magic.

It is a glow inside,

A tether that ties each soul to the source of magic and

life—the Great Magician itself.

For many, over time, it fades.

For some, it splinters, breaking off from the source.

But a few . . . a few find a way to keep it.

ALL THAT A COLOR CAN HOLD

The fall fires burned in all the parks across Vivelle, dotting the city with pockets of glow. They turned leaves to ash and sent a warm, woody aroma winding through the busy streets.

A tiny cyclone lifted into the alleyway beside Lottie, twisting leaves the color of fire and goldenrod and umber through the air, faster and faster until they blurred together. The wind stopped and the leaves settled, nestling back onto the pavement. Lottie stepped on one and smiled as it gave a satisfying crunch.

She breathed in deeply. Her nose had taken on a hint of pink in the chilly wind, but she didn't mind the cold. It only meant that winter crept closer from the north, readying itself to wrap Vivelle, the capital of the Land of the Living, in an embrace built of steaming hot cocoa and glimmering icicles and bright snow.

Each of the seasons held a special place inside

Lottie's heart. Each had its own scents, sights, flavors, and best of all *colors*. Colors she would run home and mix up until she created just the right shades to paint a scene from her day and present it to her parents. Lottie's Gallery, the long hall that separated the living spaces from their bedrooms, rotated its collection each season. It was now nearly packed to the brim with images of foliage and pumpkins, brown leather coats and hands tucked into pockets, bright red apples and acorns fallen from a tree.

Lottie's fingers itched, longing to get to her paints so she could try to recreate the way the leaves had smudged together as they spun in the air.

She peered in through the wide front window of Felicity's Enchanted Treats, a shop that was *always* crowded, regardless of the season. In the fall, they sold sticky buns and cider. In the winter, candied nuts and the best hot cocoa in town. Spring was sugar cookies and tea made from flowers that bloomed in hot water. And summer, of course, was ice cream and lemonade.

Lottie allowed her gaze to roam the line of patrons inside the shop until she found her father at the checkout, getting ready to pay. Her mouth watered and her eyes lit up at the sight of the steam rising and swirling from the cups on the counter. A treat and a walk through the park before supper—their weekly tradition was well underway.

"Ouch!"

Lottie startled as someone knocked into her shoulder from behind, sending her stumbling. She reached her hands out and braced herself against the wall of Felicity's shop, the color of which had been enchanted to change with the seasons. She could tell instantly it had been done by an artist with magic—the kind Lottie hoped to be someday. Today it was a deep burgundy that echoed the color of the remaining leaves on the line of maples across the street.

Lottie regained her footing and whipped her head around until she spotted the woman—one of the Living Gray, in a long cloud-gray trench coat and steel-colored scarf and hat. The woman tucked her neck into her shoulders and shuffled down the sidewalk, the magic inside her a faint, flickering yellow, as thin and as fragile as a butterfly's wings.

Lottie's heart hurt for the woman more than any bump to the shoulder ever could.

The people who kept their pigment and their magic glowing strong remained speckled brightly around her, moving briskly, eyes held high and filled with purpose, while throngs of Living Gray muddled slower and wearier through the streets.

Lottie sighed. How very sad it would be to lose one's

color, to have one's magic dim and fade. She touched a hand to her chest, at the warmth tucked away behind her ribs, where her own magic glowed and gleamed the color of melted gold.

Colors could hold so *very many* things. Feelings, for one. Black thunderclouds of anger or canary-yellow hope. Seething red envy or wild wishes tucked into a purple haze.

They could hold memories. Her easel set up under the falling pink blossoms of a cherry tree on a spring day, the sandy color of the crust on her mother's mixed berry pie, the coral skies at sunset on the shores of Vivelle's endless sea.

And colors also held *magic*. Everyone, everywhere, had magic, or at least they were born with it. That was just the way it was. A gift from the Great Magician, tethering the world's people to its power.

Part of Lottie's gift was seeing the color in others. Seeing the glowing magic inside them, or, if it had faded, what was left of it once they'd turned Living Gray.

"Here, kiddo." Lottie's father slipped a warm cup of cider into her cold hands.

"Thanks." Lottie took a sip, letting the tart, spicy drink coat her tongue. But something else was there too—something warm and sweet.

Her eyes lit up.

"You added caramel!"

Her father's blue-green eyes crinkled at the edges as he smiled. "If I know one thing to be true, it's that caramel makes everything taste better. Especially in the fall."

Lottie couldn't argue with him there. She mentally listed all the good caramelly things about the season. Caramel apples, caramel corn, salted caramel chocolates. A person could never get too much caramel this time of year.

"And now . . . to the park!" Her father thrust an arm up like he had just given some sort of bold rallying cry. The poorly sewn brown leather elbow patches on his tweed coat stood out even when he kept his arms at his sides. He worked hard, long hours at his job, using his gift of thinking to solve all sorts of Vivelle's trickiest problems. He knew the coat looked silly, but he'd had it forever and said it helped him think. The pine-colored magic glowing inside his chest was one of her favorite magics of all. But all that brainwork made him a bit goofy at the end of the day.

"To the park." Lottie giggled. She found her father's free hand with her own, and they waited for a break in the congestion of evening traffic before scurrying across the street and into City Greens. The park wasn't enchanted itself, though one could find enchanted things inside it if you knew where to look. From there, they would make their way home, to Lottie's mother and to supper.

THEY PASSED BY MORE THAN A FEW FALL FIRES ALONG THE way, burning in wide iron bins. A smattering of Living Gray huddled around each one, firelight reflecting off their smoky faces.

Over time, most people lost both their color and their magic and joined the ranks of the Living Gray. Some faded quickly if they faced something shocking and sudden. But for others, it happened slowly and painfully as years went by. Maybe things didn't work out for them the way they had hoped, or their dreams were deferred. A person could become Living Gray, losing both their pigment and also their ability to see color around them, from any number of disappointments. But as a person faded, one thing was certain: their magic faded, too. It was still there, but too weakened to add to the world all the beauty and goodness for which it had been created. A faded person *survived* and survived only, all thoughts of living something richer and fuller having been swallowed up by the gray.

The Living Gray could also still benefit from those who kept their magic, and from the enchanted things that magic created. But they were spectators, not partici-pants. And watching something and having it be a part of you were two very different things. Some even looked down on those who carried their magic well into adult-hood, whispering about them behind their backs like they were silly children. *Oh, what sweet dears, when will they ever grow up and join the rest of us in the real world?*

Lottie shook her head and pulled her hand away from her father's, rushing to rub at the hair on her arms that stood on end whenever her mind drifted toward sad, colorless things. Though she couldn't help it from time to time—couldn't stop herself from trying to see inside the Living Gray, to unearth what magic might be left there. To find what remained of the color that had once glowed bright inside their chests.

Hope and magic were tangled together in the most beautiful of knots, her father often said, and Lottie was certain: it couldn't be that hard to keep it, if a person wanted it badly enough.

But she wouldn't have to worry about that. She had a gift, and each day she grew in her skill and ability to use it. She had her family, her cozy apartment, her paint-filled room. Her parents had each kept their magic, and so had most of their family friends.

Nanny Nellie, who had helped take care of Lottie

for the past five years, was another story. But Lottie had grown a stubborn determination to accept her sourness as something endearing. It wasn't Nellie's fault she'd turned gray. Her tiny little glow shone the color of a clementine, plucked fresh from the tree. It would have been so very beautiful, if she hadn't lost nearly all of it when she faded. Now it only gave a small spark inside her on occasion—when she closed her eyes as a symphony built to a crescendo on a string-filled stage, or lost herself in staring at the sunset across Vivelle's skyline. It was a rare, fleeting thing.

Both Lottie and her father slowed as they approached the wide green space at the center of the park. Lottie's father's eyes—the window to his thoughts and feelings—clouded over, like they always did when they saw it.

The home of the Stone Man.

Any person who didn't know his story might think he was an art installation, a near-perfect sculpture of a man pulling his two children by the hands through the park. *How lovely*, a person might say. *What a gorgeous fixture.*

As it was, groups of people often picnicked around him, or read books on blankets, or soaked in the sun in the summer, all gone numb to what the Stone Man meant.

He wasn't an art installation, carved by an artist to add beauty to the urban green space.

The Stone Man hadn't been carved at all. He had been made.

A third option existed for the people of Vivelle. One could lose one's sense of magic and wonder, and become one of the Living Gray. One could keep one's magic and use it to make the world a better place, and see the world in color for all of one's days—as Lottie planned to. Or, though rare, upon facing a sharp and terrible sudden change in one's life, a person could grip on to their magic so tightly that instead of fading, it snapped, splintering off from its source—the Great Magician itself.

And splintered magic, separated from the source of goodness and beauty that had made it, without fail manifested into something awful. It became magic twisted into something it was never meant to be.

Lottie had first learned about it years ago, when she was seven years old.

"The Stone Man had begged his magic to help him never feel pain again," her father had told her. "But splintered magic lies. It's never to be trusted. The person whose magic splinters believes they can manipulate it to relieve their suffering in the way they think is best. But magic isn't meant to be separated from its source. It always comes at a cost, and there's always a catch."

First, the man's heart had turned to stone, slowly, over time. Then his stone heart pumped stone blood through his veins. The stone blood began to infect his organs, and he ran into the park to seek help from someone whose magic hadn't splintered, pulling his children along with him. But the stone spread like poison through his limbs, then onward to the little ones at his side.

And just like that, he would never feel pain again. In fact, he wouldn't feel anything at all.

As good and beautiful as magic had the potential to be, Lottie's father had warned her, was how ugly and bad it would get when it turned. A splinter was a ticking clock toward destruction, and those who splintered never survived.

And so even though they had to cross this part of the park to get home, Lottie and her family never came here to play. They gave the Stone Man and his children a wide berth and didn't speak again to each other until they had exited the clearing.

Lottie finished her cider and set her now-empty cup in the Reprocesser, a magical bin that compacted garbage and, using both magic and heat, transformed it into moldable, reusable material. It had been a Warwick invention, and Henry Warwick of Vivelle had been one of the best magical engineers of their time. So much so that Lottie had sat through an entire lesson devoted to him in school. But he'd disappeared over a decade prior—yet another tragic story of magic that had splintered, leaving only wreckage in its wake.

Lottie's father tossed his cup in as well just as Lottie tagged him, swiping her arm playfully across his shoulder. She gave a devious grin and shouted, "Can't catch me!" before sprinting down the path.

She didn't have to look back at her father's eyes to know the cloud had lifted. He didn't linger on sad things for overly long. His gift was to look forward, to solve problems. He spent his energy on the things he could change and he found ways to change them for the better. Right now, he was looking forward at his daughter, joining her in a game of chase.

LOTTIE'S MOTHER'S CHESTNUT WAVES HUNG LIKE A CURTAIN across her cheek. She leaned over the counter, examining a recipe torn from a piece of notebook paper. Her glasses perched on her nose and an open cookbook rested on a stand beside the stove. The warm scent of roast beef and carrots and potatoes floated through the air.

Lottie ran to her and inhaled the scent of vanilla and gardenia as she folded into a big mom-sized hug. A full, beautiful fall arrangement of flowers rested on the counter to Lottie's right: burning orange blooms surrounded by deep chocolate sprigs. *That* was her mother's gift. She could, literally, create beauty from and work magic with nature—and flowers were her specialty. She made bouquets and floral arrangements for people all over Vivelle, and *always* brought home the extras to fill their apartment.

Lottie's mother's magic glowed the soft, sweet purple of lavender.

"How was cider?"

"Good," Lottie said, pulling away from the hug and seating herself on a chair at the counter. "I beat Dad in chase."

"I'm getting old," her father said, holding his hand to his chest in fake affliction.

"Well, you'd better bolster your strength," her mother teased. "You've got an award to accept tomorrow and you need to look the part of honoree."

"They're rewarding my brain," said her father, "not my body, remember? And my brain is very ready to accept the award."

Lottie's mother laughed, a sound like fine glitter wafting through the air, then she pulled the roast out of the oven.

Her father was so good at his work that he was receiving Vivelle's Innovation Award the following night at City Hall. Lottie didn't always understand how her father's mind worked—she wasn't much like him in that way. She felt more than she thought, leaned into her heart more than her mind. And her heart swelled with pride at the thought of him winning an award for using his gift to make Vivelle a better place. Even if it meant her parents would be out late the next evening.

"Nellie'll be here when you get home tomorrow." Her mother ran a hand through Lottie's own chestnut-colored, slightly wavy hair as she gave the reminder. "You can have leftovers for dinner and you can paint for a while once you finish your homework."

"What time?" Lottie asked as her chest tightened. She was used to Nellie watching her for a few late afternoons each week, but her parents were rarely out for a whole evening. She cleared her throat. "What time will you be home?"

"I'd bet around nine o'clock, ten at the latest," her father said, joining her at the counter and sneaking a roasted carrot from the steaming plate.

"Okay." Lottie not-so-sneakily snuck a carrot, too. "But you have to promise to come in and kiss me good night."

"Of course," her mother said with a small smile as she also snatched an early bite. "But you had better be asleep."

AFTER DINNER, LOTTIE TOOK DOWN SEVERAL JARS OF PAINT from the shelf along her wall, which she would start with as her base colors. Then she grabbed a fresh palette. She got to work adding in a little here, a little there, mixing them together until she had replicated the colors of the leaf cyclone from outside the treat shop well enough to start.

She quickly fell into a rhythm, first building in the background of the sidewalk and the corner of Felicity's shop and working forward from there. The magic warmed in her chest and worked its way through her, tying her heart to her hands.

Time slipped by as Lottie worked, as the image on the paper formed and the light outside her window dimmed to dark. She swished a few final strokes, then set the brush down and lifted the painting.

Lottie's heart leapt inside her as the painted leaves flickered, then fluttered, then swirled in front of her eyes exactly as they had while she waited for her father. She could even catch a hint of the scent of cider emanating out from the enchanted painting, and could hear the low murmur of the late afternoon streets. And, like all of her art, this painting *felt* exactly like the moment she'd captured. The flurry of the city, the contentment, the comfort of a delightfully predictable afternoon.

A final painting for this season's collection. She set it down to dry and leaned back in her chair. Warmth flowed through her, pulsing in her fingertips from the use of her magic. Soon enough, she'd fall into a contented sleep.

Lottie pulled herself up and changed into her pajamas before crawling into bed. A few minutes later, her parents stopped by to tuck her in, say their good nights, and give her a kiss on the cheek.

As soon as they left, Lottie pulled a well-worn book from the shelf next to her headboard: *The Enchanted Garden*. It had been hers ever since she was a baby, a gift from her mother, and was a bedtime story favorite. The deep green cover and golden lettering winked in the light from her bedside lamp. She cracked the weary spine open and reveled in the bright illustrations. Then she read, for the hundredth, or maybe even the thousandth, time, the story of a magical garden that grew wild and free, spilling over its stone walls and spreading throughout the whole entire world. A garden that gave magical gifts and healed broken hearts.

The book started with a riddle, one Lottie didn't

fully understand. The gray words were printed in large angled letters on the center of the first page and were surrounded by an illustration of a desolate gray stone wall. Leafless gray ivy crept across the stone at all angles and nearly hid the wall behind it. It was all very strange for a book with life and color bursting from all the other pictures.

The riddle read:

THERE ONCE WAS A DOOR THAT WASN'T A DOOR,
AND A BED THAT WASN'T A BED.
WHERE MOSSY GREEN CARPET SHOT UP FROM THE FLOOR,
THIS KEY WITH THE HEART MUST BE _____.

"It's okay if it takes some time to figure out what things mean," her mother had said one night when Lottie had asked about it. That had been years ago—back in the days when they read *The Enchanted Garden* together as a bedtime story. "Sometimes answers don't come until you ask the right questions."

Lottie had nodded and snuggled into her mother's shoulder.

Truth be told, Lottie had thought about the strange riddle very rarely since, caught up in all the other more important bright and beautiful things she had to do.

Like collecting color. And collect it she did. Lottie collected color in far more than just jars of pigment or on paint-stained fingers. She looked for it everywhere, gobbling it up in books, and films, and art, and more. She breathed it in and lived it out. She drank it through her eyes. Her magic flowed inside her as easily and fully as the wind wound through the trees.

And she would never, ever let it go.

ALONE IN THE WORLD

Lottie dreamt in all the colors of the rainbow, which was the most wonderful thing in the world when she could actually fall asleep.

But tonight, the night her father received his award, she stared at the ceiling, her room dim except for the thin strip of light seeping through the space between the door and the rug. Her wide eyes blinked slowly as the sound of Nanny Nellie's heavy black shoes scraped against the floor, moving in the direction of the window, then down the hall, then to the window again.

The grand magician clock in the living room tick-tocked, tick-tocked, tick-tocked louder, Lottie was sure, than it ever had.

Nellie muttered words Lottie couldn't hear and huffed thick, exasperated breaths.

This was the very first time her parents were late to come home.

Maybe the ceremony took longer than they thought, Lottie reasoned. Or maybe they had danced the night away and lost track of time. Maybe their cab broke down by the bridge and her father was out there right now, kneeling in the street, solving the problem by changing the tire.

But a twisting turned her stomach, over and over again, no matter how many reasons she came up with that might have kept them away later than they had said. The twisting rolled into a ball, then a pit, then an ache that spread to her chest.

She took in a sharp breath and looked over at the jars of paint on her shelves, then at her brushes resting neatly washed and upright in another jar beside them. Her fingers itched, as they often did, to run over the tips of the soft bristles, to choose the perfect one. Then to pull the brush in slow, thoughtful strokes along a crisp, white piece of paper, sending a rush of goldenrod or lavender or rose into what once was empty and barren and plain. Maybe painting would calm her, give her nerves some means of escape. But the last thing Lottie needed right now was Nellie popping into her room to scold her for being up past her bedtime.

The clock struck eleven, sending long, slow chimes echoing through the apartment. The last chime lingered, its hollow, tinny note buzzing in Lottie's ears until a heavy silence swallowed the sound and settled over everything like a blanket.

Then—*bang, bang, bang*.

The pounding of a thick fist hitting heavy on wood shook the walls in Lottie's room and made the hanging pictures in Lottie's Gallery rustle in the hall. The shuffle of Nellie's feet headed in the direction of the front door, and the brisk, deep voice of an unfamiliar man cut through the air.

Lottie slipped out of bed and made her way soundlessly to the bedroom door, slipping it open with only the faintest click. Sometimes, when her parents had parties, she would sneak out and watch bright, colorful entertainers slide cards out from hidden places and make trinkets disappear. She had breathed in the scent of food created by magically talented chefs, who turned pink smoke into puffed pastries and whipped up tarts and cakes with the flick of a wrist. Her parents had once even hired someone with the gift of magical music, who had managed to play five instruments at once by herself, filling their living room with a symphony of one.

Lottie slipped out into the hall. Her back pushed against the gilded fleur-de-lis wallpaper and the tips of her toes pressed down softly on the wood floor. She slid past Lottie's Gallery, the paintings whipping into life behind her shadow. She willed them to hush.

Usually, on the nights of her parents' parties, Lottie's mother would notice her peeking an eye around the corner and wave her over for one trick, one treat, one song.

But this wasn't a party, and a stranger stood at the door.

Lottie stopped at the edge of where the hall opened to the joint living and dining space, keeping herself tucked out of sight.

It was easy to tell that the stranger was an official person on official business. Two rows of faded buttons adorned the front of his steely, well-tailored coat. He held a cap at the level of his chest and hunched over a bit, as if apologizing for something. He, like Nellie, was one of the Living Gray.

Nellie stood there, full cheeks and turned-up nose and worn, gray cotton dress. Three knobby fingers rested over her slightly opened mouth, while her other hand pressed against her stomach.

"I'm deeply sorry to bring you this news," the man offered. "It was very sudden. They won't have had time to suffer. Their souls will be journeying through the In Between, on their way to Ever After now."

The In Between. Ever After. These were places Lottie had heard about in passing, but only in relation to people who were no longer in the Land of the Living. People who had died.

Though the paintings had settled behind her, the beating of Lottie's heart, growing faster and louder by the second, threatened to give her away. She looked at Nellie, begging with silent eyes for reassurance that everything was still okay.

Nellie sighed, tipping her head toward the front window. Through it, in daylight at least, one could see the mountaintops of Ever After poking through the gaps in the tall buildings of Vivelle.

"My employers still had their magic. They lived as if keeping it were the easiest thing in the entire world. I'm told this entire apartment is saturated in color." She glanced around the room with weary eyes and exhaled, her gaze flitting past the girl peeking around the corner. "But in the end, we're all the same, aren't we? Even their precious magic couldn't save them."

The officer fiddled with his cap.

Stop. Stop. Stop. Lottie willed the word to Nellie without uttering a sound. She willed the officer to realize he had the wrong apartment and the wrong family entirely. To stick his cap back on his head and leave. She willed her parents to burst through the door laughing and ready to give Lottie her good night kiss, to half scold and half tease her for staying up so far past her bedtime.

Lottie begged from the deepest, most solemn place inside her desperate, shaking heart, to the Great Magician itself. She would do anything. She would even give up every ounce of her magic.

If only they would come *home.*

"No!" Lottie stumbled forward from the corner, losing her balance as the world grew soft around the edges. Her knees struggled to support her weight. She sucked in shallow, wheezing breaths, her lungs like balloons with hundreds of small holes poked clear through.

She caught herself on the back of a spindly dining chair and dug her fingernails into the wood.

Then, something terrible began to happen.

At first, it felt like a wave, building up over the top of the horror that had already sunk its teeth into Lottie's very soul. It lingered, its shadow towering above her for only a moment before it crested—and Lottie was pulled helplessly under.

The navy paint on the walls melted away, pooling out onto the floor and leaving them a plain, cold slate. Her wild eyes watched as the burnt-orange pillows on the couch faded, too, as if left out in the sun for ages and ages. They were quickly followed by the tablecloth, the curtains, and every single piece of art.

And her mother's *flowers*. Each bouquet faded from the outside in, the color draining from the petals first, then the leaves, then the stems.

Lottie gasped as the pale-flesh color fell away next from her fingers, spreading gray through her hands and up her arms, and injecting a shot of cold straight into her bones. Her toes, feet, and legs followed, until it was as if her body had been dipped in a bucket of dust-colored ice.

And her *magic*. The magic that warmed her from the core even on the chilliest day, the golden glow that made up *so much* of who she was pinched sharply inside her chest. It collapsed in on itself, sending a searing pain first to her heart and then to her lungs.

Some part of her tried to grasp it, like one might grasp at the roots of a tree on a cliff to keep from falling into an endless abyss. But her father's warning about splintered magic sounded off like a siren inside her head. About what could happen if she held on too tight. And so, too soon—as if she would ever be ready—Lottie felt herself letting go.

Once she did, just as quickly as the pain had started, it stopped, leaving her empty.

Lottie took in a shaking, ragged breath, and then another, and another as she searched inside for her magic's golden glow.

It was still there. She could feel it.

But the small comfort she took in the fact that her magic hadn't splintered sunk like a stone when she looked down at her chest and saw what was left: all that remained of her beautiful magic was a single speck, a sprinkle, glinting in the lamplight.

An echo, a shadow, a ghost.

For a moment, Lottie wondered if the Great Magician had heard her bargain, if she had just traded her magic for her parents. Maybe they would soon walk through the front door.

But the harsh truth grew clearer as the seconds ticked by, unmoved by Lottie's imagined happier endings.

She lay there like a pile of dirty laundry while the officer and Nellie looked down with pity at the newest member of the Living Gray. The girl who would in moments run back down the hall and rip a fistful of gray paintings off gray walls. Who would rush into her room and slam the door. Who would lie alone, smudging cold, gray tears on her cold, gray face, salty despair soaking her pillow long past the moment the gray sun rose in the gray sky.

"Oh my," the officer said. "I've rarely seen it happen in someone so young. Though I can't blame her in the slightest, after receiving this kind of shock."

"Yes, poor dear," Nellie said, her voice sympathetic and a bit uncertain. "She's got her first taste of the real world now."

And what a bitter taste it was.

AN UNCLE

Lottie had been so *certain* that it would be easy for her to hold on to her magic. Her parents had made it look simple. Lottie never doubted that she'd take after them in her own life.

But now they were gone and she was left gray. Her father had taught her that magic and hope were tangled together in the most beautiful of knots. But she couldn't hug *hope* when she fell and skinned her knee on the pavement. *Hope* couldn't fill the apartment with flowers and warm suppers, or make it feel like home just by being near. It couldn't have a weekly date with her through the park. Lottie fought against the hollow sense of betrayal that spun inside her stomach. She didn't want to be mad at her parents.

"I'm sure they didn't mean to leave you so unprepared, dear, but I don't think your parents even fully knew how to go about teaching you, not knowing themselves what it was like to join the Living Gray."

Nellie pulled up a chair next to where Lottie sat staring out the window at the mountains. She gave an awkward pat to Lottie's knee. "They didn't understand what it's like for most. Few are able to hold on to their delusions of color and magic their whole life long. Magic belongs to the children, and maybe to those who are lucky enough to float on the breeze of an easy life. It's a beautiful thing, magic is, but it isn't meant to last forever. At some point or another, we all must grow up."

Lottie frowned. Her parents had always acted "grown up," just not in the way that made wrinkles form from the corners of their lips down to their chin like Nellie.

"It isn't bad that you're gray," her nanny continued. "You've lived through loss, which is a completely normal thing. It only means that you aren't any more special than the rest."

Lottie had never felt like she was better or more special than any of the Living Gray, and she had never blamed them for what they'd become. She knew Nellie had begun to fade when her mother fell ill, and then completed her transition to Living Gray on the day she lost her. A Living Gray teacher at her school had once hoped to be a poet, but had lost the dream somewhere along the way. A family friend—someone successful in business with more money than she could ever need at her disposal—had a bad fight with her family that ended in a rift, and faded from that.

No, Lottie had never blamed them. But she *had* always assumed that the Living Gray could have kept their magic if they had just tried harder or wanted it more or put up a stronger fight to keep it.

Now that she had lived it, she knew it wasn't like that at all. It was like trying to hold on to water. Her color and the strength of her magic had slipped out through her fingers so quickly, leaving only tiny, useless droplets behind. Utterly out of her control.

If her father were here, he would have found a way to fix things, to solve the puzzle of how to make this even a little bit better. But her father wasn't here, and without him, Lottie couldn't fix anything at all.

Her mother's flowers hung their heads, falling wilted and decayed and leaving a stale, sour scent in the air. Nellie talked a while longer, her words twisting into senseless mumbles and jumbled syllables by the time they reached Lottie's ears. Then Nellie stood and removed the curled-in leaves and crumbling petals from their vases, and replaced them with the ones from the funeral. *Those* flowers were too sweet, too fresh, especially now that Lottie couldn't even see their beautiful colors. They didn't belong here.

But two of the people who did were gone. So Nellie had moved into the guest room of the apartment while some people in some room somewhere determined what would happen next to Lottie, the orphan girl, newly gray.

From time to time, someone knocked on the apartment door, whispered a few words to Nellie, then disappeared again down the hall. After, Nellie always headed back to the living room or the kitchen, and gave Lottie a tight-lipped smile that said all she needed to know.

No one has offered to take you yet.

Sometimes, Lottie wondered if Nellie might end up making the offer. She'd catch Nellie staring hard at her across the dining table, squinting her eyes and pulling her mouth to one side. But she never said anything about it and Lottie didn't pester her with questions about things she wasn't sure she wanted to know. Besides, Lottie remembered that Nellie had come to work smelling like pea soup more days than she didn't, and she could only begin to imagine the types of things lurking in an apartment that could leave a person smelling like that.

Even if it happened, living with Nellie would never feel like home.

• • •

Two weeks after Lottie lost her parents, the final leaves fell off the trees and winter rushed through Vivelle, leading its inhabitants to pull boxes of wool hats and mittens up from storage and to seal up the windows for the season ahead.

Nellie had to run out to pick up some ingredients for dinner. Though everyone knew the cold season was coming, she still mumbled complaints about the sudden change in weather from the moment she surveyed the near-empty cupboards until the moment she shuffled off to the store.

As soon as Nellie locked the door behind her, Lottie ran to the living room and opened the largest window in the apartment as wide as it would go. She was relieved to be alone. Since the funeral, she had flattened, like someone had taken a wide eraser and wiped away all the feelings her colors used to hold. Like a black hole had opened up inside her, leaving behind a gray shell in the shape of a girl.

She faced the window in her long-sleeved ash-colored dress and tights, letting the icy wind whip against her cheeks, longing, hoping to feel anything at all. Even the burn of frigid air on her skin would do the trick.

The wind snaked through the apartment, rushing into the hall and ripping several of the remaining paintings in Lottie's Gallery from the walls. Lottie watched as they wafted in the air for a moment, then fluttered to the floor, creating a path of gray memories, scattered like stones.

On a normal year, as curator of the gallery, she would have already taken down the fall paintings and stored them in her portfolio. Then she would have started in on the winter collection, which would have been mostly white with pops of things bright and bold. The red wing of a cardinal. The royal blue of a coat. The deep green of a pine.

Lottie turned away, setting her face back to the wind, to the tops of the buildings and the mountaintops beyond: the home of the Great Magician, the source of all the magic in the world. A fiery heat built up inside her, cutting through the cold like a freshly sharpened blade. She squeezed her eyes shut, but angry tears still seeped through, then quickly hardened to ice on her lashes. She wiped them away with the back of her hand, smearing slush across her cheeks.

The mountains loomed too tall, too still, too silent. What a cruel thing to take the ones she loved most in the world to a place she couldn't touch.

Keys jangled in the lock behind her. The door opened and a paper grocer's bag hit heavy on the floor.

"What are you doing, child!?" Nellie ran past where Lottie stood and slammed the window shut, setting her gloved hands to Lottie's frozen cheeks.

"I—I don't know," Lottie said, breaking her gaze from the mountains and turning toward the paper littering the hall.

Nellie's hands fell to her sides. "It's all right," she said with a heavy exhale. "Why don't you go paint me a picture while I make supper? Do you think that might be nice?"

Lottie blinked once, then nodded and sulked off to her room.

She hadn't touched her paints at all since it happened. There they sat as always on the shelves, only now they were all different shades of gray. She grabbed down a few jars at random and set them on her desk, then pulled out a fresh, thick piece of paper. She ran her fingers along the bristles of the brushes, then pulled her hand back like she had been stung.

Her paintings had been beautiful in part because of the brushes she chose, the strokes and movement and pressure, as well as the pigments. The color, the contrasts, the burst of life off the page. But mostly, they had been beautiful because of the heart that went into each one—the fact that Lottie's magic had connected her *so deeply* to the paint and brush and paper.

Without the color, without the heart, without the magic, the jars might as well have been empty.

She left her room and returned to stare out the window, where she caught Nellie sneaking a quick glance at her hands. That used to be the telltale sign—bits of ginger and dandelion and indigo smeared over the tops of her nails and the pads of her fingers. Nellie was always telling her to wash up before touching this or that and Lottie used to avoid doing it as long as she possibly could. She had *loved* carrying the colors around on her skin.

Nellie sighed.

Lottie had fallen hard from the heights of a charmed life—a warm world filled with the people she loved and rainbows of color—and emerged cold and alone and gray. Right when she needed magic the most, it had left her.

But lots of people lived the bulk of their lives as Living Gray. Now that she had hit the ground, Lottie took a strange comfort from the fact that she would never need to survive a fall like that again. A scrape on her skin wouldn't sting as bad when measured against all the other broken things inside her.

Lottie pulled a weighted gray blanket tightly around her gray shoulders. The sorrow glued her to the chair, pushed her feet into the floor, and curved her shoulders in on herself. She stared ahead with tired eyes, and a shattered heart, and an aching soul.

The heaviest, emptiest girl in the whole entire world.

A group of dark clouds gathered outside the window before bursting open and sending narrow streams of sleet falling from the sky.

At least Lottie still saw those in the right color.

THE FOLLOWING DAY, NELLIE whispered at the front door about Lottie's future for the very last time. Lottie rested in her bed, staring up at the ceiling, *The Enchanted Garden* clutched tight against her chest as mumbles and murmurs found her ears through the walls.

Soon, the door closed and Nellie's footsteps shuffled down the hall, sending echoes of the night Lottie lost her parents through her chilled bones.

Nellie entered her room, holding a folded piece of paper in her hands and wearing a cautious, tentative look on her face.

Lottie sat up and set the book beside her.

"Did you know you have an uncle?" Nellie asked, running a finger along the crease in the paper.

Lottie thought back to all the conversations her parents had had over the years. There had never been a mention of any living relative at all.

"No, I didn't."

"Well, you do. Your mother's sister's husband. Henry Warwick, of the estate Forsaken. It's a strange name for an estate, but I suppose people give all sorts of things strange names, don't they?"

Nerves lifted then prickled along Lottie's skin as she tried to put together the pieces of a puzzle she had only now learned existed. "My mother has a sister . . . which means I also have an aunt." Her heart fluttered at the thought that someone who had her mother's nose, or her eyes, or smile, might be out there, somewhere.

"You used to." Nellie unfolded the paper and glanced down at the information written on it. "She died long ago."

"Oh." Lottie's heart slowed. Her mother had never, ever, *ever* mentioned a sister. She would have remembered if she had. They must not have been close, or there must have been something that came between them somewhere along the way. Why else wouldn't her mother have told her?

Lottie had so many more questions, but the small piece of paper Nellie held couldn't possibly hold enough answers to satisfy them all.

She would have to wait until she met her uncle . . . *Henry Warwick*. Of Forsaken.

The familiar name tickled at a memory long tucked away, and a fresh wave of nerves swirled to life inside her.

"Henry Warwick, the magical engineer? The one whose magic splintered? Who disappeared into the In Between and was never seen or heard from again?!"

Nellie blinked her small pebble-like eyes slowly at Lottie. "I don't know . . . It says Henry Warwick. The name *is* familiar, but—"

"But I was taught he was dead. In *school.*"

Nellie searched the room like she might stumble on a satisfying answer somewhere along the wall or hidden in a corner. After coming up empty, she finally said, "If it is him, maybe there's more to the story than you've been taught. All I know is his name and that we're to meet his housekeeper"—she glanced down at the paper once more—"tomorrow at noon outside the last train station on the outskirts of Vivelle. The note also states that it's a long journey, and you're only to take with you what you can carry, I'm afraid."

Lottie's stomach knotted and her eyes brimmed with tears. Other than family vacations to the sea, Lottie had lived her entire life in Vivelle. Everything she loved, everything she knew, was *here.*

Lottie held her breath and pressed her lips tight in an attempt to hold in the storm building inside her from all the things she couldn't control. The truth was, she could take a thousand days going through each and every item inside the apartment, and she only had until tomorrow. How could she possibly sift through an entire life's worth of belongings between now and then and make the right choices about what was worth taking up space in her small suitcase?

No one was giving her time to say goodbye to anything, or anyone. She didn't get to say goodbye to her parents, and now she wouldn't get to say goodbye to her friends or her teachers, or the park or the sweet shop. And she was about to lose all that forever, too.

In the end, she didn't say a single word. She gave a sharp nod to Nellie, who nodded back, then quietly shuffled out of the room.

Alone once more, Lottie exhaled and fell back on her bed. Maybe she was too exhausted to think differently about it, but maybe it was for the best that she had to leave most of it behind. The things surrounding her belonged, in many ways, to a girl who no longer existed and a life that wasn't hers.

At least not anymore.

THE GRAY LADY

The sun shone down on Lottie's head as she stood on the sidewalk gripping a single suitcase in front of her with both hands. It was bright enough to make her squint, but not warm enough to make a difference, or thaw the chill inside her bones.

She used to be a bright burst of rainbow in an ocean of gray, especially at times like this when the streets were crowded in the morning and early evening hours. Lottie wouldn't ever have said she was more special than the Living Gray, but she did believe that magic itself was special. And she had loved how her magic made her stand out. She had been so certain that with it, she was meant to live a remarkable, magical life.

Now she knew better.

She watched the occasional pop of color from those who weren't gray break up the current. A powder-blue coat cocooning sunflower-yellow magic here, candy-red magic pulsing through the threads of a violet sweater there. Besides the pale flicker inside the chests of the Living Gray, it was the only color she could still see in her newly monotone world—a forceful reminder of all she had lost. If anyone noticed how young Lottie was to have faded, they didn't show it. Their eyes grazed right past her as they lifted an arm to hail a cab or greet a friend.

Lottie's gaze fell to her feet. It still stung, but in the past two weeks she had learned her lesson very clearly. She was part of what Nellie called *the real world* now

In the end, Lottie chose three items to keep, along with some clothing and a hairbrush, and a few other necessary things. Around her neck she wore a locket containing her parents' pictures, and in her suitcase she'd brought her mother's bottle of perfume and her father's tweed coat with the leather patches at the elbows.

The apartment would be closed up and sold, the money kept safe in an account for Lottie until she turned eighteen. The paint and the brushes and the pictures from Lottie's Gallery would likely be thrown away, thought of as nothing more than evidence of the whims of childhood, and not as something once most precious in the world to one twelve-year-old girl.

She even had to leave behind her favorite story. Nellie said she could only take what she could carry. And her suitcase was too heavy to carry with the book inside it. For years, especially when she was little, she had wished the enchanted garden was out there somewhere, real. But now Lottie knew that magical gardens were as foolish as the idea of being easily able to keep her magic and color her whole life long.

Bicycles swished past, a newspaper boy shouted headlines on the corner, and shoes clicked on the pavement. Cinnamon wafted from a nearby bakery chimney, heat blasted from the engines of automobiles stuck in traffic, and the sun bounced searing glares of light off patches of rain that had frozen to ice on the streets.

Nellie crossed the road and started toward the train station at a brisk clip, forcing Lottie to skitter along after her, weighted down by her suitcase. It bumped into her knees with each step, making it hard to keep up.

Huffing and puffing, Lottie slowed. Running should be reserved for people with energy to spare inside them, and she didn't really care if Nellie disappeared into the morning crowds ahead, leaving her behind. She wasn't even sure she wanted to go where she was headed in the first place, wherever that was—not that she had a choice.

Lottie paused to run the pads of her fingers along the rough, gravelly wall of the government building, a wall that had always been gray in the first place.

She pressed her palm into the cool brick while Vivelle swarmed behind her—all briefcases and suits and cups of enchanted awakening elixirs clutched in sleep-starved hands. The Living Gray called holding on to one's magic childish, foolish, and unrealistic. But they were quick to seek benefit from the magic someone else had managed to keep.

Lottie imagined the wall of the building before her giving way, allowing her to step inside it. Gray blending into gray, cold blending into cold, skin blending into stone. She imagined the world continuing on, people buzzing past on the sidewalk, not knowing that the wall had once been a girl, or that a girl was now a wall.

"For Ever After's sake, what are you thinking?!" Nellie appeared from the crowd and grabbed ahold of Lottie's arm, giving a slight pinch to her skin as she tugged her forward. "We have a train to catch, and trains don't wait."

When she was younger, Lottie used to think a train's engine was a magical machine that sent steam into the sky where it would gather into clouds—a cloud-maker. Even though she had long outgrown that particular fancy, up until two weeks ago she would have been ecstatic to take a trip on the train. Even if it was the most boring errand in the world, it didn't matter. The train, with its redwood cars and deep green fabric seats, was filled with people from all walks of life, and with all manner of dressing and sniffing and speaking. Lottie loved seeing the different magics, whether bright and bold or faded, crowded all together as she soaked up the wide spectrum of colors. Everyone had a unique story, and, on the train, those stories overlapped for one fleeting moment before bursting off in their own directions again at the station, like fragments of rainbows skittering off into the sun.

Now the cars were gray, and the seats were gray, and Lottie wasn't in the mood to see anyone's magic when hers was nearly gone. So she alternated between looking at her shoes and at the circular light that lit up as they arrived at, and then passed by, each stop. As the train drew nearer and nearer to the end of the line, the buildings became sparser, the distance between them growing and growing, until soon they had passed the farthest stop Lottie had ever visited on her trips with Nellie around town.

They hadn't talked about Henry Warwick since last night when Lottie learned he was her uncle. Nellie had to be right; there *had* to be another side to what she had been taught about him in school. Someone whose magic had splintered would have no reason to take in his orphan niece, and he clearly couldn't have disappeared into the In Between *never to be heard from again*, because *they* had just heard from him. This wouldn't be the first time in the world that the history books only told one side of the story.

Still, Lottie's nerves coiled tighter and tighter the farther they went, like a spring threatening to pop. Her fingers itched, but she crossed her arms tight against her chest to try and calm them. She couldn't very well paint to ease her nerves without the paint she'd chosen to leave behind. Instead, she kicked her legs back and forth, squeaking the soles of her shoes along the floor, matching the rhythm of the train's *chug chug chug*.

Meanwhile, Nellie fiddled with the items in her purse, uncapping her lotion and rubbing it on her hands, then pulling out her wallet and replacing it in almost the exact same spot. Finally, she took out a half-knitted scarf and started clicking the needles together as she added another row. Whenever the knitting needles came out, it was a sure sign that Nellie's own nerves had begun to fray.

"Soon," Nellie said with a flinch as she wrapped gray thread around her gray finger, speaking the reassurance more to herself than to Lottie. "Soon we'll meet the housekeeper and learn that everything will be just fine."

Lottie's heart sped up and beat like a small drum inside her chest. She stopped kicking and slunk back into her seat, watching with fearful eyes as another stop dinged on the train.

By the time they reached the last station, the houses had spread so far apart they were only dots on the distant horizon. Gray post-harvest farmland made up the breadth of Lottie's view. She had never seen the farms outside Vivelle in person, but she had often imagined them in summertime: rolling fields in shades of emerald and gold against a clear blue sky.

Lottie stared at a picture of the train line across the aisle, which now represented all the distance between Before and After on a single map. A few inches on paper, many miles along the track, and universes apart all at the same time.

They were the last ones on the train as it slowed to its final stop on the route, and Lottie could see out the window that the train station itself was also deserted—except for the ticket master and one other Living Gray lady who checked the time on a watch attached to a chain, then tucked the timepiece inside her dress pocket.

The moment Lottie and Nellie disembarked, the Living Gray lady shot a sharp glance in their direction and marched straight toward them with a determined stride. A full, round key ring hung from a loop in the woman's skirt, and it jangled and clanked with each swishing step.

She thrust out her hand to Nellie first, and observed Lottie's nanny with an appraising eye.

"I'm Mrs. Hale," she said, her voice deep and yet precise, her face polished like the silver Lottie's parents brought out when hosting a dinner party. Lottie imagined she could have stuck her face up to Mrs. Hale's and seen her own reflection inside it. But her polished exterior wasn't even close to the most interesting thing about this gray lady.

Lottie looked to where Mrs. Hale's magic should be, at least what was left of it. She squinted, searching for a hint of a spark or a tiny, flickering glow of color.

But she saw nothing. There was nothing there at all.

Lottie had never met a person whose magic had gone *completely* out. People could survive as a member of the Living Gray on the faintest remaining fleck, but she had always assumed that no one could survive it disappearing altogether.

Somehow, Mrs. Hale had. She was alive, but without any lingering magic whatsoever inside her.

The gray lady reached out her hand once more and wrapped Lottie's inside it, giving a firm, chilled shake.

Lottie took note of the woman's steely eyes framed by a high forehead, a distinctive nose, and sharp cheekbones. Each and every strand of hair was pulled back into a tight bun at the crown of her head. Not a single thing out of place.

"Nice to meet you, Lottie." The corners of Mrs. Hale's lips pulled upward, almost too slightly to be seen.

Lottie gave her just the slightest nod in return.

"You work for Henry Warwick," Nellie said.

"I do." Mrs. Hale pressed her hands against her long skirt, then folded them politely at her waist. "We understand this might be a bit of a surprising family connection."

"It was, yes. Henry Warwick hasn't been seen or heard from in years."

"Of course." Mrs. Hale cleared her throat. "It's well within your rights to seek answers, especially since you've cared for Lottie for so long. Henry Warwick, as you now know, lost his wife some twelve years ago. His magic splintered, and he used the gift of that splinter to do something no one living has ever done before. He brought about a miracle, really. His splinter has allowed him to cross through the Veil *while still alive*. Since then he's been scouring the In Between, seeking to be reunited with his beloved wife."

A crawling sensation scuttled up Lottie's spine. Her parents had never, *ever* talked about splintered magic like it was a gift. They talked about it as though it were a *curse*. Something that would lead to certain destruction and ruin every life it touched.

Lottie looked to Nellie, whose eyes had narrowed into thin slits as she stared Mrs. Hale down.

"People assumed he died when he crossed it."

Mrs. Hale gave a sharp, abrupt laugh, like Nellie had just said the most ridiculous thing, before promptly regaining her composure. "I can assure you that he is very much alive, and is eagerly waiting his niece's arrival."

"What about school?" Nellie snapped. "Out . . . there."

"She won't need *school* where she's going. And I'll take care of what she does need." Mrs. Hale's voice softened, and she knelt on the train station floor until she met the level of Lottie's eyes. "People here don't understand splintered magic, Lottie. Not *truly*. They tell the same stories, over and over again, until all people know are the times when things go wrong. I imagine that you, of all people, can understand what it feels like to have the ones you love most in the world leave you behind. The lengths you might go to if you had even the slightest hope of seeing them again."

She could. *Oh*, she could. Lottie's heart ached with how much she understood it.

"If you come with us . . . if you choose to leave Vivelle, you'll live in the In Between from now on. We won't be making another journey back for any reason. You can never return. The In Between air is deadly to living souls, so you'll be required to remain on your uncle's estate, safe inside the folds of the enchantment that protects it." She paused, and her voice took on an even gentler inflection. "But if it gives you any comfort, you'll be closer to your parents there than you could ever be on this side of the veil. And there are certain . . . possibilities in the In Between that would never be an option in Vivelle."

Options . . . possibilities . . . Lottie's entire being surged with the desire to be close to her parents again, no matter where. No matter the cost. Maybe Mrs. Hale was right. Maybe splintered magic wasn't the curse. Maybe the curse was living a life without your loved ones when you could have had the chance to be together.

"If I go with you"—Lottie darted a glance toward Nellie, then whispered, almost too softly to be heard— "do you think my uncle could find them?"

Mrs. Hale's face broke into a soft smile. She touched a hand to Lottie's arm and gave it a squeeze. "We could certainly ask him. He's out searching for Dalia right now, but you could ask just as soon as he returns."

Thoughts of the Stone Man and his children rolled through Lottie's restless mind. She looked down at her gray fingers, and then at the faint remainder of magic inside her chest. And she wondered. Losing her parents had turned her Living Gray, so maybe, just maybe, finding them might, in some way, *fix* her.

"Lottie, I'm giving you a choice." Nellie spoke with a deep determination as she turned toward Lottie with worry-lined eyes. "It's not so bad living life this way." She reached out her hand, leaving it open for Lottie to take it.

Lottie's chest constricted. She had suspected that her nanny had been on the cusp of such an offer before her uncle's letter came. But for whatever reason, she hadn't done it. She hadn't told Lottie she could stay until now.

Lottie wished she could believe what Nellie told her, wanted to trust that she'd get used to living in Vivelle as one of the Living Gray, trudging joyless and colorless and parentless through the streets. But wanting to trust something and actually trusting it were not at all the same. And the fact that she had waited until this very last moment didn't help. Maybe Nellie didn't like the looks of Mrs. Hale, or was suspicious about her uncle and his splinter, but that didn't mean Nellie actually *wanted*

Lottie. If Nellie had wanted her, she would have made it clear much earlier than this.

"Yes," Mrs. Hale echoed. "You do have a choice." She stared hard at Nellie and, too, held out her hand.

Lottie's parents had warned her so many times about the dangers of splintered magic, but everything Mrs. Hale said made it sound like her uncle had found a way to use his splinter for *good*. To fix something broken. How could a curse possibly ever do something like that?

Lottie looked back at the hazy skyline of the city she loved. It poked out from the flat horizon like a mountain made of iron and glass and steel. All of her memories were tied to the places inside it.

One way or another, she would have to learn to live with ghosts. But there was only one place where she could potentially reunite with them as well.

She took Mrs. Hale's hand.

Nellie's arm dropped to her side. "Are you very sure, then, Lottie?"

Lottie tried to say something, but her throat had dried out. She settled for a curt nod instead.

"All right, then." Nellie's shoulders slumped a bit more than they usually did, and pewter tears pooled in the corners of her eyes. But she found a way to say goodbye.

Too soon, Nellie headed back to the train and gave a final, fake-cheerful wave as she boarded. Lottie watched as her nanny took a seat that faced away from where she and Mrs. Hale stood. And she didn't look back again.

Lottie hated that she had just become another loss in Nellie's life. It hurt almost as much to realize that Nellie was now another loss in hers.

Lottie had made her choice, though she couldn't quite escape the creeping sensation along the back of her neck as it all sunk in. She had shut the door on a life in Vivelle forever, and there would be no turning back. But she couldn't see a single path out of her sadness besides this miraculous chance to be near her parents, to maybe even be together with them again. She could say goodbye to a lot of things if it meant the possibility of that.

"Time to go, Lottie." Mrs. Hale took another peek at her timepiece before moving briskly toward a set of wide doors marked EXIT.

Lottie adjusted her grip on the suitcase as they passed the hot steam pouring out of the front of the train. She watched as it lurched forward with a weary *chug chug chug*, then picked up speed, heading back to the colors and lights of the heart of the city.

Then she followed Mrs. Hale out of the station and farther away from Vivelle.

THE IN BETWEEN

In front of the train station stood something unlike anything Lottie had ever seen. Black from top to bottom, it most closely resembled a carriage, a form of transportation that no longer existed in Vivelle—except for those who paid to tour the city that way. Only instead of wheels, this carriage-like thing had *legs*. Eight of them, bending outward before curving to the ground, like a mechanical spider. It whirred and bobbed up and down, as if it were actually breathing.

Lottie slowed. "What is it?"

"It's a Beast of Burden, of course." Mrs. Hale stopped and sized up the mechanical wonder. "I'm sure you must at least be familiar with your uncle's skill set."

"I am." Lottie stepped forward to the Beast and peered inside the window. "But where's the driver?"

Mrs. Hale patted Lottie on the head. "Your uncle's magic built this, dear, just for you, to retrieve you from the train. We don't need a driver. It drives itself." She clicked the door open and offered Lottie her hand.

Matching the outside, the interior offered squeaky, shiny black leather seats and black velvet along the walls surrounding the near-panoramic windows. Mrs. Hale handed Lottie her suitcase, then joined her on the seat and shut the door.

Lottie set her suitcase down at her feet, then ran her fingers along the fine velvet. It was, without a doubt, the smoothest thing she'd ever touched.

"If you're impressed with this, just wait until you see the estate." Mrs. Hale pulled a small bag containing a sweet roll out from a satchel beneath the seat and handed it to Lottie. "I thought you might be hungry."

Lottie took the roll and set it in her lap as the Beast started to move. Its curved legs scuttled out of the station, rotating in a perfectly timed rhythm that made the ride surprisingly smooth.

"Do you want to split it?" Lottie pulled apart the roll and offered her half.

"No." Mrs. Hale flinched a smile. "I'm not hungry."

Lottie set the roll back on her lap and ate it very, very slowly, wondering if she'd ever eat a roll like this again. If the food in the In Between would be very different from the types of things she was used to eating in Vivelle.

Meanwhile, the Beast maneuvered onto a quiet gravel lane. From there, Lottie watched as they ambled on for miles and miles, until the farmlands turned to empty, uncultivated fields. Farther than she ever knew the Land of the Living even went.

Lottie finished the roll, then fiddled with the fabric of her skirt between her fingers and stared at the rambling nothings outside her window.

"Do you know why my parents never told me about him? My uncle?" she asked, breaking the long stretch of silence.

Mrs. Hale paused and tipped her head back and forth, as if weighing how much to say. "I think, in the end, your parents weren't quite as brave as you are, Lottie. Your aunt died only weeks after you were born. Your mother and she were very, very close. Warwick offered for them to join him when your aunt passed so you could all find a way forward together. But they didn't trust your uncle's splinter, and I suppose they thought it would be safer for you not to know about him at all." She sighed. "Such a tragedy, really. That a man's search for his wife could tear a once-close family apart."

Now it was Lottie's turn to weigh Mrs. Hale's answer. If that really was what happened, and if her parents had made a different choice back then, she would have spent her whole life in the In Between. If she hadn't ever known Vivelle, all of her experiences, all the things she'd come to know, would have been so very different.

But though her parents were fearful of splintered magic, it made sense to Lottie that they would choose to stay in Vivelle for another reason as well. Her mom hadn't been Living Gray; she had never faded, despite losing her sister. Maybe Mrs. Hale had gotten that part of the story wrong—maybe they actually hadn't been close, like Lottie had first thought. Or, maybe they had been, but her mother didn't feel like she needed to leave Vivelle and find her sister to be whole. She had new baby Lottie after all—a full, rich life to live, right where she was. Maybe she didn't want to leave it behind.

Meanwhile Lottie had nothing, and so she was leaving nothing behind. It hadn't been hard to make her choice.

After what felt like hours had passed, Lottie caught sight of something wavering through the air, almost how the pavement on the road looks in the distance on a blistering day. As if the air itself was moving—like a thin, transparent veil.

Throughout her whole life, Lottie had hardly given the In Between any thought at all. She knew it was the space where the souls of those who died transitioned before they eventually ended up at the mountains of Ever After, whose distant peaks she'd seen so many times through her window back home.

She knew the In Between existed in the same way she knew that factories on the outskirts of Vivelle used to dump chemicals into the water that caused all sorts of problems for people downstream, or that sometimes boats capsized at sea. She knew it in the way she knew that bad things could happen, or even heard about them happening to other people. The whole idea of the In Between felt so far away and irrelevant. That was, until something bad actually happened to her.

But now she was here. *It* was here. Real. The In Between. About to change her life. They were moments away from driving straight through the border separating everything she'd ever known in life from the Land of the Dead.

"Say goodbye to the Land of the Living," Mrs. Hale said plainly, as a ripple of hunger passed over her eyes, like a person staring down a feast on a grumbling, empty stomach.

Fear spread its icy fingers from Lottie's gut straight on out to her tips and toes. The only thing that kept her from screaming and begging to turn back was the thought playing over and over again in her head—

Her parents were in this place.

Her parents were in this place.

And she was about to be there, too.

Lottie closed her eyes and pictured them in her mind. Her father's crinkle-cornered eyes. Her mother's warm smile. She'd made a way to be where they were. Next, she would find them. And it would help fix things. It *had* to.

Living life with even the ghosts of her parents had to be better than living without them at all.

Lottie tightened her grip on the side of the seat as they began to cross over, passing through the thin, wavering curtain. She clenched her jaw and braced herself as a rugged wind smashed into the Beast of Burden, nearly tipping it sideways.

She lost her hold and tumbled toward Mrs. Hale, who sat stiff and still, completely unaffected.

"Such a thin veil that separates us," the woman said, her voice flat and haunting. "They all think we're worlds apart, when it is but a thin, thin veil."

Inside the car, the air shifted to something somehow even colder and drier than the winter air in Vivelle. Lottie gripped her skirt tightly. She barely dared to blink as a new landscape took shape before her. A place so strange that she didn't think she would have ever imagined it to be like this, if she had ever thought to try.

Dry, cracked soil stretched out endlessly on each side, framed only by the farmlands behind the veil they had just crossed, and the mountains of Ever After far, far beyond. Short, spindly, leafless trees speckled the flatlands, their branches like upside-down legs pointed toward the flat-toned, cloud-covered sky.

"It looks a little like Vivelle," Lottie offered, desperate to pull on any thread of something familiar. "The leaves have just fallen off our trees, too. We were waiting on the first fall of snow."

"The seasons belong to the Land of the Living, dear," Mrs. Hale said matter-of-factly. "In the In Between, it's always like this."

Lottie's eyes filled with unexpected tears. She had loved the seasons so, so much. The traditions of them, the scents, the decorations. The *colors*.

She tried to tell herself that it didn't matter. That, as Living Gray, the seasons would have been soured for her anyway. That she would have to learn to accept the fact that here there would be no snow, no spring, no thaw.

Still, it was a loss. One she would add to the ever-growing list of things now gone. And, yet again, she hadn't been given the chance to say goodbye.

Mrs. Hale pulled a tissue from her pocket and held it

out toward Lottie. Lottie took it and wiped her eyes, then her nose, then took a slow, shaky breath.

The In Between may not have any seasons, but it did hold one thing in abundance that Vivelle didn't have at all.

And that was the ghosts.

Lottie squinted at the masses of souls traversing the In Between. Beings shaped like people but not quite solid, in pants and shirts and shoes and dresses, all headed to the mountains. Mrs. Hale had said she could find her parents in this place, but Lottie hadn't realized until now what the souls of the dead would look like. No one had talked or speculated much about ghosts in Vivelle.

Some of the spirits ran, their gray legs pumping fast beneath them. Pure longing and hope spread across their ghostly faces, like they couldn't wait a second longer to reach Ever After. Others moved more slowly, like they didn't want to rush, and seemed a bit unsure. They even passed by a few who stood still, their faces twisted and burdened, like they were working through some private feelings that left them stuck in place. Some of the ones who weren't moving forward had gathered and formed tiny, ramshackle encampments out of rotting wood and odds and ends the wind had blown in from the other side of the veil. It reminded Lottie of the clusters of solemn-faced Living Gray that dotted the park in Vivelle as they huddled around a fall fire. The thought made her shiver.

"Why are some of them not moving to the mountains?" Lottie asked.

"All sorts of different reasons." Mrs. Hale leaned toward Lottie's window. "Many aren't sure Ever After's the kind of place they want to be."

"But isn't it good? Ever After?"

Mrs. Hale shrugged. "I wouldn't know. I've never been. Have you?"

Lottie scrunched her eyebrows together. Of course she'd never been.

She turned back to the window.

Many people had complained that Vivelle was growing too crowded, that there wasn't enough room on the streets for a person to truly breathe. But it had always been easy for Lottie to find quiet, peaceful spots off to the side of the ruckus. Vivelle had always had plenty of room for her.

But here, in this new land, they passed *so many* ghosts on either side, pressed in on one another, it put the complaints about Vivelle to shame.

"You'll get used to them." Mrs. Hale tipped her head. "Living where we do. The walls of Forsaken are lined with enchanted hemlock, which keeps them out. Wouldn't want to find someone who doesn't belong wandering the halls in the darkness. No. The only way for a ghost to get inside Forsaken is if they've received an invitation, which is what you'll give to your parents. Just as soon as your uncle finds them."

Lottie nodded, but she didn't really need the reassurance. She wasn't afraid of ghosts.

A gray girl was a soul in a different kind of transition than the souls in the In Between, as she learned to carry the weight of great sorrow on her shoulders. She didn't care how morbid or strange it was to imagine reuniting with her parents in this place, because it gave her the first bit of comfort she had felt since the moment her world emptied of color. And if she could find comfort anywhere, even in the idea of living among the dead, she was going to take it.

In fact, she thought she might belong more in the In Between than she ever could have if she had stayed behind in Vivelle.

Because she was only half alive herself.

FORSAKEN

"You can start to watch for them now, if you want to," Mrs. Hale said. "Pretty soon you'll be bound to the estate like the rest of us—for our own safety, of course. But not to worry. Your uncle will have the best chance of finding them and sending them to Forsaken's gate because his splinter allows him to travel freely. Though you never know. They may pass close enough for you to spot them first." A light, almost like a single flicker of a flame, danced in the gray lady's eyes as she said it.

The idea that at any moment she might pick out her parents' faces in the sea of ghosts, that at any second she might get them back, jolted Lottie like a strike of lightning straight to her heart. It reanimated her with an energy she'd almost forgotten she could have.

Lottie understood that her uncle had been searching for his wife for years, and that finding her parents might take time. But their reunion could also be as close as her next breath, and she would hold tight to that possible outcome, too.

Lottie watched and wondered at the souls with renewed determination—the running ones, the walking ones, and the ones standing strangely still or huddled together around a meager encampment. She watched for her parents and willed herself not to blink so she wouldn't miss them as they passed. She kept her eyes open until they burned, until pools of wetness gathered in the bottom; then she squeezed them shut, letting tiny, ice-cold rivers stream down her cheeks. They quickly dried to a path of thin, dusty frost that she wiped away before continuing her search.

Until the Beast of Burden shuddered.

"What was that?" Lottie ripped her gaze from the window.

The Beast lurched forward, kicking up a trailing cloud of dust behind it, and the muted daylight outside began to dim.

"The magic," Mrs. Hale said calmly, though a deep crease formed in the space between her brows. "It's wearing thin." She let a tight exhale escape her mouth as she touched a finger to her chin. "I can't imagine it could be much farther."

She and Lottie exchanged one more glance. Darkness overtook them and the ghosts blended into the night. A few more minutes passed in silence as the Beast scuttled shakily along.

Then, out of the black nothing, a shape, a shadow, something darker than all the rest, rose up a short distance ahead. A shadow resembling a castle, topped by a beacon of light that swooped and cut through the night like the lantern of a lighthouse at sea.

"Ah, there it is." Mrs. Hale flicked imaginary dirt off her skirt with the tips of her pointy fingers. "That's Forsaken. We're almost home."

Lottie fixed her eyes ahead and tried the word on for size in her mind.

Home.

No. She had lost *home* the minute that officer came to the door and told her the horrible news. She had lost home when she realized her life would never look the same. When her world went from filled with parents who loved her and bright, popping color to empty shades of dreary, wretched gray.

This was the place Lottie would live, but there was no reason to believe anything would ever feel like home again.

That was, until she found them.

• • •

GRAVELLY ROCKS CRUNCHED UNDER THE BEAST'S LEGS AS IT slowed. A set of black iron gates swung open, the path ahead of them lit by only the occasional swoop of light from the beacon above.

Lottie watched the gate swing closed behind them with a sharp, heavy clank. She couldn't be sure, but it seemed as if two huge stone statues of winged angels that had looked down on them as they entered had somehow turned their heads, and now also watched them pull up the drive.

The movement itself wasn't surprising. Vivelle was full of enchantments like that, but they were usually whimsical or playful in nature—a mannequin might tip his hat to those passing by, or a gargoyle might blow bubbles out its mouth that tasted like sugar when you caught them on your tongue.

But nothing at all felt playful about the winged angels at the gate and their cold, empty eyes.

The Beast coughed and sputtered as it slowed to a stop next to a set of stone steps. The steps led up to a thick wooden door, nearly three times Lottie's height. On each side of the door, gas lanterns sent flickers of light and shadow stretching against the walls.

"Just in time." Mrs. Hale threw the carriage door open and hopped down. Lottie grabbed her suitcase and did the same. The Beast shook and hissed, then collapsed into pieces right there on the drive as if some giant had mistaken it for an actual spider and smashed it with its foot.

Once fallen, the carriage dissolved into a pile of blackened ash while dozens of lingering screws and springs bounced and spun across the gravel.

Lottie watched in horror as the remaining pieces continued to move long after they should have stopped—first bending, then squirming, transforming from metal to *alive*.

In moments, what once was a grand and luxurious magically engineered Beast of Burden had dissolved into dozens of tiny maggots and oily worms seeking shelter from the spotlight. They burrowed into the driveway headfirst, then disappeared into the ground.

A wind kicked up, sending the remaining ash up and away into the sky, and then all fell quiet.

"What was that?" Lottie asked, her voice trembling.

"The magic got tired," Mrs. Hale said, unaffected, as she led the way up the stairs.

Lottie lingered behind.

Splintered magic lies, her father's warning echoed in her head.

Lottie shook it off, told the voice to be quiet, and scurried after Mrs. Hale.

The wooden door creaked open on its own power, as if sensing their arrival, and the gray lady and Lottie stepped inside.

There, Mrs. Hale grabbed a white candelabra, with long drips of creamy wax frozen in place down its sides. She lit it with a nearby match.

"There's no electricity, but I'm sure you'll find an abundance of other familiar comforts," she said as she led Lottie down halls that were as silent as death and as dark as tombs.

Finally, she clicked open the door to a cavernous room and ushered Lottie inside it.

"This will be your bedroom," she said, shooting an unimpressed look around the space. "Forsaken is quite large and the night gets very, very dark. It's best if you stay put until morning so you don't get lost. Bathroom's through the door next to the bed. I'm kept busy with my work for your uncle most of the time, so you'll primarily be in the care of Agnes, who helps out with the house. She's left a bit of a snack and some water for you on the table. She'll be back with your breakfast at seven, and then she'll show you the way outside so you can continue your search."

The last part she said with the enthusiasm of someone certain that Lottie would succeed in her task.

It bolstered Lottie's confidence even more, and she offered a small smile back. This might not be her home—not yet—and Mrs. Hale might not exactly be her friend, but she had traveled a long way to bring Lottie here, and she had given her hope.

Mrs. Hale wished Lottie good night and shut the door. Once alone, Lottie found the embers of a fire pulsing slowly in the hearth and a lit candelabra that gave her just enough light to see by, though it faded to black near what Lottie presumed was a very high ceiling.

She was used to feeling small in Vivelle. There, she was a tiny piece of a huge puzzle, crowded in among all the other pieces. A part of a larger, busy, buzzy whole. And she had *loved* it. But here everything was big, and dark, and empty, which made for a very different kind of feeling small.

Lottie clutched the locket around her neck, then pressed its cold metal against her chest before letting go. She opened her suitcase, removed her mother's bottle of perfume, and set it next to the candelabra. She tipped her nose to it and inhaled. Then she took out her father's jacket and breathed it in, too. She didn't know how long they would smell just like her parents, but relief surged through her at the fact that they still did for now.

She sat at the table and ate some of the snack Agnes

had left for her—some dried fruit and salted crackers—then went to the bathroom and brushed her teeth in the dim, flickering light. She rested her toothbrush in an empty silver cup on a counter next to the sink once she was finished.

Back in her room, Lottie found a salt-colored nightgown with a ruffled collar resting on top of a monstrous canopy bed. She put it on, then cocooned herself in her father's jacket and climbed under the covers.

In a building that looked like it had never held a single child inside its cold stone, the walls of her room were, in fact, covered in faded tapestries depicting children in sorrowful situations. One girl sat in a lonely corner next to a pile of dirt and a broom. Another walked through a forest with the shadow of a wolf following close behind her. A third lay asleep in a glass coffin in the middle of the woods.

What bizarre pictures. Never in a million years would she have dreamed of using her art to create such unsettling scenes. But, back when she painted, she had also never experienced any sort of unsettling things herself. Maybe whoever made the tapestries had.

The frozen faces of the children stared down at her, and Lottie scowled back at them until the candle dripped down to nothing and the embers of the fire faded to black.

Her locket, holding gray pictures of her lost parents inside it, burned her skin with its cold. She pulled her father's jacket even tighter around her shoulders.

There wasn't any possible way she could search the In Between for her parents at night, but she still couldn't help but feel she was somehow wasting precious time.

Between thoughts of people taken too soon, and legions of ghosts trudging forward, and colors lost forever, Lottie finally fell into a fitful rest.

SOMETIME DURING THE NIGHT, AS LOTTIE LAY IN UTTER darkness, a great groaning jarred her awake.

She opened her eyes and shuddered as the groaning rumbled through her and shook the room to its core. Even the bedframe trembled, like it was lying at the epicenter of a massive worldquake. Lottie's breathing grew faster and faster, then tighter and tighter inside her chest as the walls shifted against each other, grinding like stone teeth, like the deep growl of a hungry ogre who fed on scared little girls in the night.

And there was something else, too. Something beyond the groaning, or maybe even *inside it*. The sound of someone crying. The same kind of wailing, desperate sound she'd made in her room on the night she lost her parents. The groaning wrapped around the crying,

AGNES AND GEORGE

A thin seam of gray light peeked through a gap in the dreary room's thick drapes, slicing through the darkness and landing on Lottie's nose. She had finally fallen into a deep, dreamless sleep when the light caused her to stir.

Her hair spread all around her head in tangles and gnarls, angry from all her tossing and turning. A stale, sour taste rested on her tongue. She unwrapped her covers, shrugged off her father's coat, and crawled out of bed, landing on the cold wooden floor. She padded over to her suitcase, grabbed a pair of wool socks, and pulled them onto her feet. She paused at the tapestries and, in particular, at the children woven into the fabric.

They had moved overnight within their respective tapestry scenes. One girl had shifted from the corner with the broom to a window seat to the right. The girl with the wolf behind her was now skipping instead of walking. The one in the coffin was now sitting up and wearing a strange smile. And their eyes all gleamed, full of mischief.

Lottie frowned at the children and shook off a shiver. She *had* just moved into a house run by a man whose magic had splintered. She'd have to get used to the fact that the enchanted items inside must have been swallowed up by the splinter, too.

She walked to the window, pushed the heavy curtains aside, and peered out at the world below. The mountains of Ever After stood closer than she'd ever seen them.

Lottie exhaled, creating a hollow space in the front of her chest. There were so many things she didn't understand about Ever After and the vast, barren wasteland of the In Between that separated it from the Land of the Living. So much she would have to learn, and a lifetime living in the Land of the Dead to do it.

To start, she could see that the ghosts were kept out of the grounds of the estate by a tall brick wall with a series of sprigs tied an arm's length apart all along it. That must be the enchanted hemlock that kept out the spirits who didn't have an invitation.

Inside the wall, Forsaken contained a series of smaller walled gardens, or what might have been gardens, once upon a time. Empty spindling branches of shrubs and trees crowded together in corners, and frosty grass, with blades sharp like scissor tips, poked through patches of cracked soil.

Lottie blew a tepid breath across the window, creating a foggy circle, then turned away and glanced once more around her room, checking to make sure the tapestry children hadn't moved again while she wasn't watching. She noted a few editions of dusty old children's books, a desk, a chair, and a small table—all gray. Other than the bed and the dresser, which, like everything else in her world, were gray as well, they made up the entire contents of her room.

Overall, Forsaken gave off the impression of a cursed castle, with the life inside it strangled by something evil, just before spring brought the snowless winter to a thaw. Lottie tried not to think about the blank-eyed angels at the gate or the maggots or the groaning and crying she'd heard in the night. She would live in a place like this for a thousand years, if it meant she had a chance to find her parents.

Now, to get herself outside.

A thick silence sat both inside her room and beyond it in the halls. There wasn't even the clank of dishware or the click of a heel or the echo of a voice to be heard. Nothing at all to indicate that other people were near.

Lottie drew her arms around herself. Mrs. Hale couldn't just leave her in this room without knowing where anything or anyone was forever. She had mentioned someone, a girl who helped with the house.

Of course, the girl would come. But Lottie couldn't entirely brush off the fear that she had been forgotten. She had lived all her life just assuming that people who left returned. Now she knew that sometimes people—even the people most important to you—could be gone forever in an instant. The thought emptied her yet again. Before all of this, she had never known that emptiness could rest, heavy as lead, inside a person's core. But it could. And sometimes it made it difficult to stand. And at times, to even breathe.

Lottie startled as the door clicked open behind her. A voice spoke, bright as the bubbles in a bottle of fizzy drink, breaking apart the deep quiet.

"Good morning! Oh, I didn't mean to frighten you, dear."

A girl, almost a young lady—a splotch of color in the middle of the gray—entered Lottie's room wearing a blush pink dress and crisp white apron. Both the magic glowing inside her chest and her cheeks matched the pink, and her light brown hair was pulled back in a ponytail. A few curly strands had set themselves free and framed a strikingly friendly face. The kind of face most people couldn't help but smile back at.

Most people. Not Lottie. Lottie stared back at the girl without so much as a muscle twitching. She didn't know there would be people like *her* here, still with all their magic and color.

Lottie crossed her arms and gave a little stomp, which didn't punctuate things as well as she'd hoped given the fact that she only had wool socks on her feet. Just minutes ago she had been hoping someone would come for her, and now someone had.

But she would have much preferred Mrs. Hale. At least *she* didn't have any magic at all to flaunt in Lottie's face.

Undeterred, the girl reached back into the hall and pulled in a wooden cart on wheels with a hearty gray breakfast on a tray. Two warm biscuits sat on a plate beside a heaping scoop of scrambled eggs and a pile of buttery breakfast potatoes, accompanied by a tall glass of milk. She strode forward with heavy, slightly clunky steps, like she wore shoes too large for her feet, then lifted the tray and set it on the small wooden table.

"I'm Agnes." The girl wiped her palms on her apron and stuck out a hand and grinned. "Hale's too busy with her work for Mr. Warwick, so you'll be mostly seeing me."

"Lottie." Lottie lifted her hand limply, just enough

for Agnes to take it and guide her to the table.

Lottie scowled at the breakfast. The food here was familiar, at least. But she couldn't bring herself to eat it. Her stomach sat small as a pebble inside her.

"Not much of an appetite, huh?" Agnes stared at Lottie with a curious expression. "When we're feeling sad, sometimes it can be hard to eat, at least for a while."

"I'm not sad," Lottie said, her lie carrying a sharper edge than she meant. "I'm going to find my parents. I just need you to show me how to get outside."

"I see." Agnes's shoulders slumped. "Hale did say I should help you bundle up and send you out into the yard. Though she didn't say *that* was the reason."

Agnes wasn't nearly as enthusiastic as Mrs. Hale, but Lottie didn't care to stick around and learn about what this magic-filled girl thought of her plans. She'd head outside, straight to the brick wall, and climb on top of it. She'd sit there and scan the ghostly faces for a hint of something familiar. And when she saw them, she'd call out, and they'd turn back toward her and then everything that was wrong would be right again—at least, as right as it could be now.

Agnes stepped out as Lottie changed into a pair of pants and a sweater. She also found a coat and boots and hat and gloves in the dresser, and put those on as well.

Agnes gave a small frown when she returned, which led Lottie to believe that the winter gear had pigment while they were folded and had faded as she pulled them on her own wiry frame. The Living Gray had not only lost their own color, but they also had the power to drain the color from the things they wore around their shoulders and on their hands and feet.

Finally, Agnes grabbed a long, knitted scarf and wrapped it around Lottie so many times that it covered not only her neck, but also her chin, mouth, and the bottom of her nose. As soon as she stepped back, Lottie yanked the scarf down and glared.

Agnes stifled a laugh in return.

"There." Agnes patted Lottie's shoulders after re-wrapping the scarf a bit lower around her neck. "That'll do." She placed a finger over her lips. "Now we need to hold our tongue in the halls, as the sound magnifies terribly and we aren't to be a disturbance."

Lottie didn't like being grouped as a "we" with Agnes, or the thought of them needing to do anything together, even if it was just being quiet in the halls. But she didn't know how to get out on her own, and she also didn't want to get into trouble. She'd just have to follow Agnes and all her pinkness for now, at least until she didn't need her help.

Oblivious to Lottie's irritation, Agnes gave a kind smile, lifted her skirt, and led the way down a series of halls, some lined on one side with tall, narrow windows that faced the mountains. The echoing of their boots against the dusty floor was the only sound or movement in a vault of stillness and quiet.

They passed suits of armor whose necks creaked as their heads turned, and galleries of paintings—all dreary landscapes and sorrowful portraits. They also passed dozens upon dozens of closed doors between sets of twisting stairs. Lottie couldn't help but imagine what kinds of things might be hiding behind them. One day, once she'd found her parents, she'd have time to explore.

Her apartment in Vivelle had been small enough to cross in less than a minute. But here, Lottie followed Agnes for what felt like forever before they reached a side door tucked away in a lonely looking corner.

Agnes opened the door, and a sharp, nipping air bit at Lottie's nose, taking her breath away completely. She slunk her nose and cheeks back under her scarf until she looked like a turtle.

"Off you go," Agnes said with a giggle. "I'll ring the bell for lunch. Hale says you can stay out until then."

And with that Agnes waved Lottie off with a smile

that created deep, crater-like dimples in her flushed cheeks.

Lottie turned away and marched along the side of the house, as much to keep warm as to get away from the too-cheerful girl. Her feet stomped on hundreds of brittle, frozen blades of grass, crushing them beneath her. Shattering them like glass.

She'd been so distracted by her mission that she'd completely forgotten to ask Agnes about the groaning she had heard in the night. She would have to remember to ask when she saw the girl again.

Lottie turned a corner and grimaced as she found herself face-to-face with yet another blot of color in the shape of a person. A gardener, with dark blue overalls and brown boots and magic the same color as his faded denim shirt. Lottie's magic hadn't splintered, but the fact that the little bit that remained allowed her to still see the magic inside others felt a bit like her own kind of curse.

And there were too many pigmented people here to remind her of it.

The man removed his hat to scratch his head, revealing white hair as fluffy as cotton candy.

"You must be Lottie." He replaced his hat and gave a soft, slightly somber smile.

"Yes."

"It's nice to meet you, Lottie. I'm George."

George leaned on his pitchfork and they stood in silence, each staring at the other for a moment until George's gaze flickered to the few rows of turned dirt that stood between them, all filled with robust plants. A pile of fat potatoes and a smattering of thick carrots sat in a wheelbarrow next to his feet.

Lottie bent to the soil and ran it through her fingers. She hadn't seen this garden from her window—probably because it was too close to the side of the house. "I didn't think any of the gardens here were alive. Things don't usually grow in the winter."

"That's true," George said. "But you could say I've got some skill in the way of growing crops and tending to the animals in the barn round the back side of the estate. And my wife, Lydia, transforms all this into what you see on the plate, with her own kind of gift in the kitchen."

George bent down and pulled up a long, crooked carrot, then tossed it into the wheelbarrow. "And I'd be sodden if I couldn't get things to grow, even in a place like this." He winked, then gave a sober glance straight above them, to where a tall, circular tower perched high above the rest of the estate. That must have been where the beam of light came from last night as she arrived.

Lottie followed George down the row, weaving around fat heads of cabbage and leather-leafed vines.

"Do you know," Lottie asked, "the quickest way to get to the outside wall?"

George set down the wheelbarrow and his eyebrows pulled together. He rubbed his fingers along the stubble on his chin. "Now why on earth would you want to climb a wall that looks out on a sea of ghosts?" He sized her up once more, this time through a thick cloud of sadness.

Lottie looked away from the eyes that searched her face. She didn't know what he was hoping to find there, but she didn't need two people in a row to tell her they disapproved of her plans.

"Ah," he said, seeming to have found what he was looking for anyway, though he didn't seem surprised. "Do you know what makes a good day for me, Lottie? A full one? It's if I can look down and see I've got dirt under my fingernails as night falls. If I've used my gift, done a good day's work, and found a way, however small, to make the world a better place, then I go to bed happy."

Lottie didn't understand what George was getting at, but she definitely understood what it felt like to need to do something with her hands.

"I used to paint," she said, the words erupting from her before she could stop them. Even at the mention of it, Lottie's hands itched for the comfortable familiarity of her brushes and the feeling of stroking fresh paint along a crisp page. The longing spread through her, enveloping her, tempting her with memories of the wonderful, magical warmth that used to unfurl from her heart straight out to the tips of her fingers.

No.

Lottie opened her hands, pulling her fingers taut and as far apart from one another as possible. Since that terrible night, the images in her head had all turned sad and gray. Nothing she would want to put onto paper and bring to enchanted life on the page, even if she still had enough magic to do it.

She stared down at her splayed fingers.

She needed to get away from these colorful people. She had to find her parents.

"I know you've endured a great loss, Lottie," George said, as if sensing the change in her. "But it might not be wise for a young girl to spend so long looking for the dead, even if she thinks it might be the only way to recover what's been lost."

A searing heat rose up from Lottie's chest and flooded her chilled cheeks. What could any person who still saw the world in full color possibly understand about loss? She tried to blink them away, but icy tears pooled in the bottom of her eyes, moments away from falling.

"Oh, I didn't mean to upset you," George said, his voice heavy with real regret.

But it was too late. Lottie was off, stomping her cold boots away from George and his garden, away from the man who couldn't possibly understand what it was like to have the ones who meant the most in the world to you snatched away, without warning.

It was a weird word George had used, but Lottie was pretty sure *she'd* be "sodden" if she listened to his advice. She'd find the outermost wall, climb to the top, and look for her parents in every single face of every single ghost, as long as she liked—all day if she needed, all week if it made her happy.

As long as it took to find them.

THE FROZEN TREE

Lottie stomped along the paths between several walled gardens. Prickly gray vines crawled up the sides of the stone like skeletal claws. She turned, corner after corner, until finally, she spotted the wall that formed the barrier between Forsaken and the In Between. Then a bone-deep sound stopped her in her tracks.

The grating of stone against stone while Forsaken groaned against it.

Lottie's stomach twisted.

It was happening again.

Just like overnight, the entire estate grumbled and shook. But this time Lottie lost her footing and slammed against the frozen earth. She turned on her knees and covered her head with her hands, even though it wouldn't do a lick of good to protect her if the garden walls fell. She'd be buried alive or broken to pieces.

This time, though, there wasn't any crying along

with the quakes. And just as quickly as it began, the groaning stopped. Silence flooded the grounds once more.

Lottie waited—

Nothing.

Relief flooded through her as she pulled herself to standing and dusted ice crystals off her knees. Whatever the groaning was, it was over—at least for now.

And there, just ahead, stood a narrow brick staircase leading to the top of the outermost wall. The stairs were set in the space between two large sprigs of enchanted hemlock that stood tall and upright against the wall like guards made of gray pine.

Lottie would be able to see the ghosts from here for sure. Her heart fluttered like the wings of a butterfly dancing through the air. From here on out, at any second, she could find her parents.

She ambled up the stairs and sat down at the top, surveying the In Between and the mountains from a new and closer angle. A flat blanket of clouds still settled in the sky above her, but at the cusp of Ever After the clouds broke, revealing a sunlit sky beyond. Even in Forsaken's chill, Lottie didn't wish for the sun now like she once would have on a dreary, cloudy day in Vivelle. She shifted her weight and settled in. Now she belonged more in the cold.

So many souls in transition passed Lottie by as she sat and searched; souls that had lived well into old age, and younger ones, with a few children, too, among them. Most of them running, and walking, others moving forward one small step at a time . . . all going to Ever After—a place she had heard was filled with love and peace. At least, she'd grown up hearing that from people *other* than Mrs. Hale, who didn't seem as certain.

From her vantage point, Lottie scanned the ghostly figures for the silhouette of a woman in a beaded gown and a man in a black tuxedo—the clothes her parents had been wearing on the night they died.

No sign of them yet. But Lottie was determined to keep looking. No matter how many ghosts she had to sift through along the way.

THE LONGER LOTTIE SAT SCOURING THE SOULS FOR ANY SIGN of her parents, the more she realized that time seemed to move rather differently in this new place. In fact, in the space between the Land of the Living and Ever After, time wasn't an easy thing to keep track of at all.

Days passed. Then, eventually, weeks. The groanings that had populated her first hours at Forsaken had stopped. When exactly, she couldn't say. Hours blended together, each day beginning and middling and ending exactly the same: Agnes brought breakfast, Lottie bundled up, then went outside and sat at the top of the wall looking for her parents until lunch, and then after, again, until dark.

UNTIL ONE MORNING, AT AGNES'S INSISTENCE, LOTTIE tucked a biscuit in her pocket before heading out.

"Remember what I said." Agnes wrapped Lottie's scarf and repeated the same words she spoke every single day. "About chasing ghosts."

Lottie nodded as always, but once outside she went straight for the wall that overlooked the In Between and climbed the narrow brick stairs.

The fact that she couldn't leave Forsaken gnawed at Lottie from the inside. It had started early, like a small, persistent itch she couldn't scratch, and only gotten bigger and itchier as time went on. Maybe it would have been better if her magic *had* splintered. If it had, she would have made the same exact wish as her uncle, and she wouldn't be stuck here on this wall, hoping her parents would come near enough to Forsaken for her to spot them. She'd have been able to use her splintered magic to search the In Between herself.

A nasty voice inside her whispered that she was ridiculous to think she could ever find them. After all, her uncle had been searching for years, even with the advantage of his splinter.

Another voice whispered that it would all be fine. The In Between was vast. Looking for her parents was like trying to isolate a single star without a map of the sky. She shouldn't expect to find them quickly.

Lottie kicked her heels against the wall, slow at first, then faster and faster as the whispers sent their unsettling, dissonant messages swirling through her mind.

She searched until her eyes grew weary, and the ghosts began to blur together. She searched for so hard and so long that she almost missed a bright blot of color when it flitted past the corner of her eye.

Lottie snapped to and turned toward it. There she found a cardinal, its feathers a deep and fiery red, circling above her. The cardinal landed on the wall a few feet away and cocked his head, as if questioning Lottie's presence. Lottie cocked her head back at him. After all, if anyone looked out of place here, it was the bird.

"Hello, Cardinal," Lottie said, as gently as she could. "I know what you're thinking. But you're the one who looks like you don't belong here, you know. You're much too bright. We're all gray here . . . Well, the estate is gray. And some of the people."

The cardinal tipped his head the other way and

fluffed his feathers, showing off, like he didn't care in the least if he stood out.

Lottie couldn't help herself, the corners of her mouth lifted, just a bit, at this funny little creature. She reached into her pocket, pulled out the biscuit, and broke a few crumbs off into her palm. She sprinkled them on the top of the wall between them, then held her breath, not hoping too much, but not wanting to ruin the moment and scare him away, either.

The cardinal eyed up what Lottie offered, let out a happy trill, then hopped over and pecked at the crumbs with his beak, making quick work of the little snack. When finished, he turned his beady black eyes up to her. He opened his beak slightly, maybe an attempt at his own small smile of thanks.

If this had been Lottie's normal life—her life before the unthinkable happened—and she had seen the cardinal in Vivelle on a walk in the park on a white winter's day, she would have painted his portrait. She would have caught this exact expression on his face and framed him in snow-covered branches, then displayed the picture in Lottie's Gallery. And each time she looked at it, she would have smiled at the thought of her little bird friend.

Yes, she would have done just that *if* life had been

what it used to be. Still, even here in her gray body on the gray wall in the gray estate, she softened to the feathery little creature. For some strange reason he had decided to pay her a visit from wherever he called home, which couldn't be anywhere near here.

"I like you," Lottie whispered to the bird, surprising herself with the truth of it. She hadn't liked much of anything in a good long while. "Would you like to stay for a bit?"

The bird hopped closer until he was right next to Lottie's side, as if to say *I like you, too* and *Yes, I'll stay*. He followed Lottie's gaze as she looked back at the ghosts and they watched a few minutes together in silence.

Then, without warning, the cardinal soared up into the sky, twirling in the air before flying over the grounds of the estate.

Lottie turned to watch him.

Her gaze skittered past the barren trees that poked their gangly limbs out the top of dozens of walled gardens, all void of life, and the fallen branches that littered the paths where decaying leaves cowered in abandoned corners.

And Forsaken stood tall above the wasted ground. Jagged cracks crept up the stone, and black rot darkened splotches at its edges. The single, round tower rose high above the sad yet stately house, so twisted and crooked it looked like it might fall off entirely and come crashing if the wind blew the wrong way. The wide window that faced the mountains stared at Lottie like a single, unblinking eye.

The cardinal twirled and spun, tempting her gaze away from the tower, daring her to keep sight of his dance in the air. After a few moments, the bird landed on the topmost branch of a sprawling tree inside one of the walled-off gardens. One Lottie hadn't yet noticed from the window of her room, which held a limited view, or the top of the wall, from which she was almost always looking out, away from the estate.

And she gasped at the sight.

All the trees in the In Between were barren, but this tree was *different*. Ice glistened off the blackened branches of the tree the cardinal had chosen, like they had been coated in clear glass.

Lottie's heart caught in her chest.

Maybe this was why the cardinal had come: to show her the way to this garden.

Lottie climbed down the stairs and rushed to where the bird had landed. She passed other gardens, some with doors shut tight, and others with wide open archways that led inside, but when she came to the garden that she was certain contained the cardinal, all signs of the bird had disappeared.

And there wasn't a door to be found.

The wall of this garden was lined with hemlock sprigs tied between thick curtains of leafless ivy that crawled up the stone. Undeterred, Lottie pulled at the ivy and peeked behind it, searching for a way in. But the ivy pushed back, working to fill in the gaps Lottie tore open almost as fast as she made them, like it was annoyed by her presence and didn't want her to peek.

The embers inside Lottie flared once more. Forsaken had twisted, splintered magic, and secrets hidden in the shadows. But she was a girl who had lost everything precious, and she was going to find out what was behind this ridiculous wall.

She tore at clumps and clumps of ivy, until, even through her mittens, her hands stung from wrapping her fingers around the brittle stalks.

But still, she kept trying.

After a while, hidden behind a particularly stubborn patch, so knotted and tangled she couldn't see past it until she moved it aside and held it there with every single bit of her strength, Lottie found a small hole.

She held back the ivy with one arm. It curled around her wrist and poked at the exposed skin between her sleeve and her mitten, pinching her in an attempt at distraction. She pushed back on it even harder. Then she brought her eye to the circular gap between two stones, noting the stale, sharp scent of charred wood as it wafted through.

Most of Forsaken looked abandoned and forlorn, stuck in an endless, snowless winter.

But inside these walls lay a spread of ice encasements and drooping, frozen decay, like an ice storm had swooped in just as the garden was dying and covered everything till it glistened. Shriveled gray ice-encrusted flowers posed at the end of frozen shoots along the frosted garden floor. The ice and the stillness, well, it almost looked like . . . *magic*. Like the garden had been literally frozen in time, cast under a strange sort of spell.

Somehow, despite how it appeared, and in a way she couldn't exactly explain except as something like a hum, or a beat, or a song, Lottie felt the pulse of the garden through that tiny hole. Like somehow life remained, hidden under all that ice and spoil. It tickled at a memory, something from her life back in Vivelle. A gray page, with a gray stone wall and gray ivy forming a curtain all around it . . .

THERE ONCE WAS A DOOR THAT WASN'T A DOOR,
AND A BED THAT WASN'T A BED . . .

Her book. *The Enchanted Garden*. One of the so many things she left behind. The garden in that book hadn't had a door either, at least not one that was easily found.

In fact, the wall of this garden looked exactly like the wall on the first page of the book. The one with the riddle she'd never quite understood.

She had read that first page many, many times in her old life but now, being here, severed from the world she used to know and the things she had once loved, only random, disconnected words flitted through her head. Letters danced up next to each other before floating away, flipping and spinning. And then they were gone.

Green, carpet, key.

The riddle had a line about a key. But she couldn't remember what it said. Her mom had mentioned something once about needing to ask the right question to find the answer.

Lottie pulled back from the ivy and clenched her fists. A longing to be close to her parents in any way, big or small, surged inside her. She had her locket, the smell of her mother's perfume. She wrapped herself in her father's jacket each night. And now there was this.

Maybe it was silly, but this was the first garden she'd ever met without a door. The book had been a gift from her mother, and this was her mother's sister's house. Maybe her mother had known of this place. Maybe it had been special to her, too. Maybe, somehow, the story Lottie had read so many times was a bit more than just a story.

For someone who wanted so little since she lost her parents, other than to be reunited, Lottie now wanted something else very badly. She wanted to find a way inside.

"Hello!" she called out. "Mr. Cardinal, are you there? Can you show me how to get in?" She waited, listening for any rustle of movement.

Nothing.

"Please?" she called again.

Still, nothing.

Lottie shouted once more and waited for something, anything to happen.

She didn't know how long she waited, still as could be, while the silence both stretched out and pressed tightly in around her. But she didn't move until the jingle jangle of the lunch bell wound through the path, landing on the ears of a Living Gray girl who stood with clenched fists outside a frozen, doorless garden.

Alone as ever before.

A FIERY HEART

The heat that had crept up her face on the day she first met George had long settled back down to a simmer in her stomach, but now it billowed like a breathed-upon flame.

She clomped back to the door, yanking on clumps of vines and kicking her boots against the walls a few times for good measure as she went.

"There you are, Lottie," Agnes said as Lottie stomped past her. "I didn't see you at the top of the outer wall today. Did you find a different spot? Or . . . something else to do, perhaps?"

Lottie stopped in her tracks and snapped her head toward Agnes. In all the days she had sat at the top of the wall, she had thought she was alone.

"You've been spying on me?!"

"I only check in on you through the third-floor windows while I clean." Agnes lifted her arms, palms up, as if offering Lottie something she couldn't see. "I'm sorry but it's . . . not *natural*. Children should be playing, not staring out at a field of ghosts."

"You sound like foolish, ridiculous George." Lottie seethed as the heat flared inside her once more. She balled her fists and tore down the hall, turning left then right, running up stairs and down them, until she had gotten herself completely and utterly lost, backed into a doorless, stairless corner.

Why, today of all days, could Lottie not find *doors*?!

"Lottie!" Agnes shouted after her, panting, breaking her own rule of silence in the halls as she scrambled to follow.

Meanwhile, the fire inside Lottie continued to grow. It burned like a bonfire, starting in the pit of her stomach and now spreading its flames through her chest, down into her legs and across her arms—pulsing searing heat. She tore at the curtains framing the large window at the end of the hall and screamed.

"Leave me alone!"

"Shh! You have to be quiet! Hale—" Agnes reached out, brushing her hands against Lottie's arm. Lottie slapped them away, not caring if it stung.

"What do you know?!" Lottie shouted, her throat tight as the sound screeched out of her. "You don't know anything about anything! So what if I want to find them?! They're *my parents*. It's the most *natural* thing in the world for me to want them! I didn't even get a chance to say goodbye!"

Lottie fell to the floor and kicked her legs and thrashed her arms so hard against the stone she was sure they'd be sore when it was over. But it didn't matter. Everything inside her was ice and fire, swirling and surging and forcing its way out through tears and screams and pounding limbs.

Between her screamings, Lottie peeked at Agnes, only to find that she stood calmly to the side of the hall, waiting for it to be over, patient as could be. She might as well have been waiting for a loaf of bread to finish baking in the oven.

The fact that someone could stand by with such composure while her insides were about to burst irritated Lottie even more. She kicked and thrashed, over and over again on her back, then on her stomach, then on her back again, slamming the floor with her fists for a good long while and kicking the boots off her feet while she did it. She kept going until she had rid herself of the storm, until the flame inside her died back down to embers. Lottie hiccupped as her breathing slowed and she stared up at the ceiling.

Empty.

"Are you finished?" Agnes asked, her tone less bubbly and more resolute than Lottie had ever heard it before.

She didn't feel like answering. So she sat up and wiped several strings of hair off her sweaty face, pressing them back into the rest of her head. Her hat and mittens lay strewn at her side.

"I like you, Lottie," Agnes said, her voice measured and even. "Though Ever After knows you aren't making it easy. But I'd ask you to tread with more care in the future. For one, you're not to throw fits like this in the halls. Second, I know you must miss them something awful, but searching the In Between for ghosts isn't healthy. Even if you think you're doing what you're doing for the *best* of reasons. And third, you can't know what a person's been through just by looking at them. With that in mind, I'd ask you to be a bit gentler toward George—my father."

Lottie snorted. It was completely obvious what she'd been through when people looked at *her*. And it was obvious that Agnes, and George, in all their color and all their magic, were completely fine. "You wouldn't know what it's like," she said with a pout as she crossed her arms over the front of her knees. "You aren't Living Gray."

Agnes wrung her hands together. "Just because

a person has their magic and their color doesn't mean they've never known sorrow or that they don't know anything about loss."

Lottie stared at Agnes, and Agnes stared back. She rested her folded hands in front of her apron, patient as ever, as if she could stand there for hours waiting. As if it wouldn't be the least bit of trouble, even if it took the entire day.

Lottie's muscles were as limp and weak as soggy noodles, and she could just about curl up and take a nap right then and there on the cold floor. But her stomach grumbled, loud enough for Agnes to hear.

Lottie gave a sharp huff, then stuffed her boots back on and gathered her hat and mittens. She gestured for Agnes to lead the way to her room. She wouldn't talk any more in the halls; her throat hurt from all the screaming anyway. Though Agnes couldn't stop her from stomping her feet.

But before they could take a single step, the groaning overtook the house again, making the hall and the floor shudder. Lottie and Agnes both braced themselves against the wall as they fought to stay standing.

Agnes's eyes grew wide and her mouth fell open like a fish, like she had been caught in a situation she had hoped to avoid.

"What is this?!" Lottie yelled over the rumbling of the great house. "What's going on?"

The quaking and the groaning roared as loud as the empty belly of a beast, just as it had the other two times.

The sound of someone crying out pricked at Lottie's ears over the din of the quaking.

Then Mrs. Hale's voice cut through all the racket, sharp as a blade.

"Agnes! You're needed this instant! Agnes!!!"

"I'm sorry," Agnes said to Lottie, "it'll stop in a moment. Head up the stairs and to the left when it's done. You'll find your room there. I have to go!" She took off down the corridor, disappearing around a corner and leaving Lottie alone in the rumbling hall, her gray fingers clutching at the curtains.

THAT EVENING, AGNES ENTERED LOTTIE'S ROOM, DINNER tray in hand, well-prepared with answers meant to placate a curious, frightened girl.

"The house moves," she said as she poured hot water into a pewter teacup. "The groaning you hear is the house relocating to follow your uncle as he searches the In Between for Dalia's ghost. I'm sorry, I thought Hale would have told you."

Truth be told, Mrs. Hale hadn't told Lottie much, but

at least Agnes's explanation made sense. Her uncle and Forsaken were probably tied together by some invisible cord, connecting his magic to the estate.

"But what about the crying?"

"The what?" Agnes froze, her eyes as wide as if someone had shone a light on them, catching her in the middle of doing something sneaky.

"The crying that sometimes starts up when we move."

"Oh, that." Agnes set down the pot of tea. "Of course. Sometimes it sounds like a person crying when the wind whips around the corners. You'll get used to it and then you'll see. Everything's fine." Her voice softened. "Completely and entirely fine."

Lottie couldn't help but notice the shift in Agnes's tone when she said those final words, like she was trying to convince herself as much as Lottie.

"But I heard someone crying," Lottie insisted. "Someone crying while Forsaken groaned."

"But you didn't," Agnes said, her words final. "It was only the house moving and a fearsome wind."

Lottie turned toward the black night outside her window. She wasn't a stranger to the kinds of sounds the wind could make. Maybe in the In Between, the wind was somehow different, but back in Vivelle at least, she'd never heard wind that desperate and sad.

HENRY WARWICK, THE SPLINTERED

Late that evening, just after Lottie had drifted off to sleep, Mrs. Hale burst through the door, brandishing her candelabra.

Lottie startled, then sat stick straight up in her bed.

"Your uncle's returned!" Mrs. Hale exclaimed in hushed excitement. "But he won't stay long, just enough to gather fresh supplies. If you want to talk to him, now is your chance. Well, what are you waiting for?! Get dressed, child!"

Mrs. Hale finally took a breath and Lottie's brain worked to catch up with the abrupt arrival of new information.

Her uncle was here. *Now.*

Lottie scrambled out of bed, threw on some socks, replaced her father's jacket with a sweater, and attempted to smooth out her hair. Her heart beat so loud she was sure Mrs. Hale could hear it.

This was it. This was what she had been waiting for. To ask her uncle to use his magic to help her find her parents.

"I'm ready."

Mrs. Hale smiled a most gracious smile.

Lottie hadn't been out in Forsaken's halls at night since the evening she arrived, but unlike then, when she didn't know what to expect from her new life, she had now grown more comfortable with the estate's various types of darkness.

Instead of taking the stairs that would lead them outside, Mrs. Hale turned, leading Lottie in the direction of a heavy door—the entrance to Forsaken's tallest tower. The bottom half of the door was thick and studded with iron, while above it a series of metal grates covered a wide rectangular window like bars on a prison cell.

The usually closed and bolted door now stood open, and Mrs. Hale's candelabra threw a warm flicker along the walls framing a set of narrow, curving stone stairs.

Mrs. Hale's shoes clacked sharply as they ascended. Lottie followed, skirting around corners draped with cobwebs and speckled with dozens of fat spiders that scuttled into deep cracks in the stone at the disturbance. They passed by a small, darkened alcove to the side of the stairs, then climbed higher and higher, until Lottie's legs ached and her lungs burned.

A subtle glow from the top of the tower brightened as they finally spilled out from the stairs and into a small, circular room.

And there, in the far corner, stood a peculiar man—the only family Lottie had left.

Lottie knew that when a person's magic splintered, it would do so shortly after they began to fade—when they could feel their magic slipping and chose to grip it tightly instead. She had felt this herself when she learned that her parents were gone, before she remembered her father's warning and let her magic go.

As expected, her uncle was Living Gray. *Deeply* gray, like mountainside stone.

He was a man composed of sharp angles, and sunken features, and eyes tucked back in their sockets like dull black buttons. A faded black cape hung limply from his back, his simple clothes sagged on a gaunt frame, and his unkempt raven-black hair covered his ears like a dirty mop. He bent over a glowing scroll that started at the top of a slanted desk and unrolled across the entire length of the room.

Maybe anyone who didn't have Lottie's particular ability wouldn't be able to tell the difference between him and the rest of the Living Gray. But Lottie could see what was inside him. His magic wasn't completely empty, like Mrs. Hale's. And it wasn't a faint, barely there fleck like her own, either.

No. Henry Warwick's magic had splintered.

And now it *smoldered* inside his chest.

It breathed like the hottest part of a fire, where the flames fanned white, and blue, and violet.

Lottie pressed her back against the wall. She grabbed at the rounded corners of the cold stone and swallowed a scream. Even the room smelled of burning things— swirling ash and glowing flame and suffocating thick smoke.

She knew with certainty that she had never before met anyone whose magic had done *this*. She would have known if she'd met someone splintered. And she would have run.

Mrs. Hale placed her hand on Lottie's shoulder. If she knew what Lottie could see, she didn't show it. And she certainly wasn't afraid.

"Henry," Mrs. Hale said, catching his attention. "Your niece is here."

Lottie's uncle startled, then smiled. The kind of thin, gaunt smile you might expect from a skeleton come to life inside a nightmare.

"Hello, Lottie! It's about time we finally meet! So glad you've joined us on our glorious adventure. Mrs. Hale said you had something to ask me before I head back out, and I told her to bring you to me right away."

Though her muscles and her heart told her to run out of this tower as fast as she could, her uncle's voice gave Lottie pause. Despite his frightening appearance, the words that came out of the man standing before her were kind in nature and warm in tone. Even a little bit fatherly, in a strange sort of way.

She released her hands from the wall.

"It's all right, Lottie. You're safe here to share your heart," he said. "You see, Mrs. Hale is my angel, and if she brought you to me, then it must be very important." A string of spittle connected his top lip to his bottom as his mouth hung open like a broken hinge. "She showed up on my doorstep the day I lost Dalia, with a broom in one hand and a plan in the other. She heard my heart, right when I needed her most. And she's made a way."

Mrs. Hale lowered her gaze. "I've lost someone, too," she said softly. "I understand very, very much the sting of this kind of pain."

"She's your angel, too, you know," Warwick continued. "When she learned you were an orphan, she's the one who suggested I take you in."

Lottie looked to the gray lady. "I didn't know that."

"Of course you didn't. Mrs. Hale is as humble as they come, but it's the Great Magician's honest truth."

"But how did you find me?" Lottie asked. She hadn't even thought to ask the question before now. When her parents died, people scoured Vivelle for any living relative who might take her in. But the one who did come forward was from *outside* Vivelle.

"The Ledger of Souls, of course!" Warwick exclaimed, his voice rich with barely contained excitement. "Come and see."

Lottie stepped forward toward the man with the smoldering, splintered magic. Heat radiated out from his insides like a human furnace. Lottie coughed as the scent of smoke caught in her throat. But her need for answers outweighed any uncertainty or hesitation.

"On this scroll is the list of every soul traversing the In Between at this very instant. The names appear the second a soul crosses the veil from the Land of the Living to the Land of the Dead. Mrs. Hale acquired it for me. Isn't it marvelous?!"

Lottie searched the list of glowing names, all written in angled cursive, like from an old, magic quill. Her eyes caught on a pair, one right below the other.

She touched her fingers to them.

Garrett Michael Burnett

Elizabeth Carlyle Burnett

Her parents.

"Can you find them?" Lottie asked, her voice shaking. Their names glinted even brighter against the glow from her uncle's magic, like a mirror in the sun. "I've been trying from here, but I can't leave like you."

Her uncle leaned over the scroll and touched his fingers to the names, too. They stood there for a moment, gray next to gray. Grief next to grief. Loss beside loss.

Then he looked Lottie right in the eyes. "Of course I can."

And everything that had bound itself up so tightly inside Lottie while she'd waited for her uncle unraveled at last. This had been her mission. Her single quest. The thing that tempted her enough to follow Mrs. Hale's invitation into this ghost-laden place to begin with.

A silver tear slid down Lottie's cheek.

"Do I have time to show her?" Her uncle turned to Mrs. Hale with eager, hopeful eyes.

Mrs. Hale paused a moment, then pulled out her pocket watch and snapped it open. She smiled, though her words carried a slight hint of tension. "Of course."

"Wonderful. Then come here, Lottie. Follow me."

Lottie pulled herself away from the scroll and its

glowing names, then followed her uncle and Mrs. Hale back down the stairs.

They turned into the darkened alcove Lottie had passed on her way up. Only it wasn't an alcove at all. She walked through the doorway and into a strange room that looked like it belonged to a mad scientist, or, in this case, a splintered magician.

Pipes and tubes connected to beakers and burners on a counter. Different liquids stood in dozens of glass vials on a series of wooden shelves off to the side. Stacks of books teetered in tall, messy piles all around them. And in the room's center, a huge tangle of round, toothed cogs and wheels—some as tall as a small house and others as tiny as a coin—created a massive, overlapping, intersecting display. The gears connected to a set of wires and tubes that merged at a glass vat nearly filled to the brim with a black, inky substance. And, near the very top of the imposing structure, a long lever stuck out from the machine's side.

Warwick walked confidently forward. His large Adam's apple bobbed as he leaned over the monstrous, mechanical contraption.

"Do you know what this is, Lottie?" Excitement flickered over his face and his splintered magic flared a deep, fiery red.

The scent of salted tears and despair and decay lifted from the vat and saturated the air around them. Lottie shook her head.

"It's *sorrow*. It's all of the sorrow of all the people on this estate, those who have enough of it to spare. I gather it here and convert it into energy in this very tower, like a rain cloud gathering moisture. The In Between is vast, but this allows Forsaken to come with me, to follow along as I search. I ration the pace with this lever, but, as you can see, we have plenty to go around, in part thanks to you. In fact, when you arrived, you actually helped to create this abundance."

"You might not have known it at the time, but the choice you made that day at the train station had momentous, wondrous implications." Mrs. Hale stepped forward and set a sturdy hand on Warwick's shoulder. "Had you stayed in Vivelle, dear, your sorrow would have been wasted. But here, it holds great value."

"It has *purpose*," her uncle added.

"Indeed."

Lottie had never once thought that something good could come out of the terrible thing that had happened to her. But if what they said was true, then her sorrow had *meaning*, and it was helping to do something important and good. Even though she couldn't leave Forsaken herself, she would be helping her uncle to find them. Any remaining echoes of her parents' warnings about what comes to those who harness splintered magic, and to those who draw near to it, faded like mist rising from the sea at dawn.

"Thank you," Lottie said. "Thank you for showing me this."

"Of course." Warwick looked at the vat of sorrow, then at his machine, like a proud, doting parent.

Mrs. Hale snuck another quick peek at her watch.

"And now," he said, "it's time for me to go."

"But it's late." Lottie peeked out the room's only narrow window. "And it's dark."

Warwick inhaled deeply through his nose and lifted his chin, his sunken, black eyes steeled with purpose. "As long as my mission lies before me, I don't need sleep. Just a bit of water, a bit of food."

Lottie ambled after her uncle as he descended the stairs. He grabbed a hat off a table in the hall and tipped it toward Lottie, then swung around, sending his cape billowing out behind him. He lifted a bag of supplies from against the wall up and across his shoulder.

"Don't worry, Lottie. The darkness doesn't scare me."

The front door opened, and her uncle disappeared into the night.

THE CRYING HALL

Lottie had barely gotten herself settled back into bed when Forsaken shook and groaned again, making the floor beneath her bedposts rumble. But, for the first time, she smiled as it started, because she understood that the house and its magic were following her uncle out into the In Between. And that the very sadness inside *her* was helping him in his search.

Her parents were closer than ever before, she was absolutely certain.

She glanced around the room quickly before shutting her eyes, but not before noticing the tapestries had changed again. Now the faces of the girls were all frozen in an expression of utter horror. They stared down at her, eyes wide and mouths open in a silent scream.

Lottie stuck out her tongue.

Then the crying started again, too—a desperate wailing that snuck through the gaps in the doorframe and the cracks in the walls.

Lottie scrambled out of bed and ran to the window. She pressed her ear against the frigid glass, testing if she had actually confused the sounds of the wind and the house for someone crying, like Agnes had said. But like the woven faces of the children on her walls, the outside world was silent, too.

When the groaning died down and the wailing, this time, continued, Lottie knew that Agnes had lied. What she didn't know was *why*.

Lottie clicked her bedroom door open and peered out into the hall.

The meeting with her uncle had left Lottie feeling brave. She had splintered magic on her side and in her corner. And if the wailing wasn't the wind, then it had to be coming from *inside* the house.

Lottie set her jaw and lit her candelabra and entered the hall, drawing a long shadow behind her. Her stockinged feet moved soundlessly on the cold floor as she turned this way and that, trying to find the source of the sound.

Lottie walked and turned and turned and walked as she followed the wailing, backtracking when it got softer, and walking more quickly as its volume increased. She passed through eerie, silent rooms with furniture draped in white sheets. Then, a butler's pantry, with dusty half-drunk bottles capped with cracked corks, like they had been abandoned in the middle of a party. Even a small theater with a worn wooden stage and torn leather seats.

One room stood completely frozen in time, the furniture uncovered and coated in dust—a lady's room for sure. The faint scent of perfume still lingered in the corners, and a set of moth-eaten dresses hung in the closet. Even in the stagnant air, Lottie recognized vanilla and gardenia. She paused a moment and closed her eyes as she breathed it in, the same perfume her mother used to wear.

She continued to follow the cries, crossing paths with twin gargoyles framing the banister of a staircase. They shifted and creaked to follow her as she walked, and their sharp-toothed mouths drew back in a scowl. Torches along a narrow hallway flickered on and off like street lamps, as if warning Lottie to slow down or turn away. She traced a dripping sound to a puddle on the floor beneath a painting of a beautiful woman whose eyes were crying real, paint-stained tears.

Lottie's heart pinched as she reached out a finger to touch one of the tears. Her own paintings had come to life because of her special magic, which had been much brighter and more hopeful than this. More than that, even the air around this painting felt heavy and weighted, with a gravity all its own, all bleak agony and wretched despair.

She shook her head, snapping herself out of the painting's pull, and continued on her search.

Finally, when she was nearly on top of the crying, a door opened and a stream of light poured out into the pitch-black hall, casting the silhouettes of two women against the floor. Lottie blew out her candles and ducked behind a corner, where she could watch the shadows without being seen.

"He can't continue like this." A woman's voice spoke at just above a whisper.

"I can't *make* him stop." Mrs. Hale's voice, crisp and sharp, didn't reciprocate the other woman's attempt at quiet.

"I know what he said, but maybe we could just introduce him to Lottie. She's not *un*pleasant. Maybe it would cheer him up to have a friend."

Lottie now recognized this voice as Agnes.

Mrs. Hale shut the door firmly, and the darkness swallowed their shadows whole. "Hush!" she snapped. "I've told you he wants nothing to do with her. Not a word. Not a mention. He must be left *alone*."

Lottie frowned. Whatever was going on in that

room, it sounded like *whoever* was inside it didn't want to see *her*.

Agnes sighed.

Lottie listened as the sound of their skirts shuffled away down the hall.

She waited until she was sure the coast was clear, then she tiptoed to the door and touched her hand to the knob. She didn't know what she would find, or who might produce such sad, desperate cries. Or why he didn't want to see her. But she did want answers. And she wanted them now.

Lottie turned the knob, pulled the door open, then slipped into the room. Compared to her own cavernous space, this room felt too small, too packed-in-tight. Heavy drapery covered every square inch from floor to ceiling, except one wall lined with thick dusty bookshelves, spilling over with books. A large canopy bed with velvet curtains filled almost the whole floor, and a wide wooden dresser with a clutter of items laid out on it took up nearly the rest. The air in the room tasted like dust and things gone stale and sour.

"Are you a ghost?" A small, childlike, wavering voice spoke from behind the curtain.

THE HIDDEN BOY

"N o," Lottie said, taking a small step forward as she tried to get a better look. She squinted her eyes, but she couldn't see anything through the narrow gap in the curtain surrounding the bed. "Are you?"

"No," the trembling voice answered from the shadows. "Who are you?" The voice spoke a bit bolder this time, a bit clearer, but still with the lightness of a child at its core.

Lottie exhaled, relieved, then took another step. "Can I . . . can I see you? It's tough to talk to a curtain."

The voice hesitated, then responded, "Okay."

Lottie stopped in front of the bed and pulled aside the fabric. There, under a thick, downy quilt, lay a boy. A gray boy, who looked about her age, with inky-black overgrown hair and the same deep, smoke-like gray skin as Lottie. Fine beads of sweat lined his forehead, probably from the fit he had just thrown.

The boy's chest rapidly lifted and fell, and a curiousness emanated from his expression, in the lift of his eyebrows and in the shape of his eyes and their irises black as night.

"I'm Lottie," she said. "I live here. Henry Warwick is my uncle."

"I'm Clement," the boy said. "I live here, too. I'm Henry Warwick's son."

"His son?" Lottie asked. The hair on her arms stood on end.

"Then that makes you my . . ." The boy sat up, and the blanket covering him fell. Beneath his pajamas Lottie saw a weak hint of grass green magic blinking inside his chest.

"Cousin." Lottie completed the thought. But that simple, straightforward word broke something open in Lottie's heart. She had been told that she was the very last living branch on a dying, splintered family tree.

And now, sitting here before her, was a *cousin*.

Clement lifted his chin, a bit less affected but surprised just the same. "I didn't know I had a cousin. No one ever told me about you. Why." He spoke that last word more as a command than a question.

"I don't know. No one told me about *you*, either. And I've been here several weeks now."

"But . . . what are you doing here?" Clement asked.

"My parents died and Mrs. Hale picked me up. I'm from Vivelle."

Clement leaned away from Lottie. He tilted his head and frowned. "And you *agreed* to come?!"

"Mrs. Hale said I could find my parents . . ." The words rushed out of Lottie, swift as a stream. "I didn't have anyone else in the whole entire world. I was alone."

"Ha!" Clement laughed and fell back on his pillow.

Lottie scowled, about ready to head back to her room and pretend she'd never come here at all. "It isn't nice to laugh at someone's sorrow."

Clement took a deep breath. "I'm sorry. But sometimes I have to laugh or I might fall into a pit so deep I'd never climb out."

Lottie had never tried laughing to help her through anything that had happened, but she'd definitely tried plenty of other ways to cope. She'd stared out her window in front of an icy wind, unable to move. She'd searched for her parents, given up everything she'd known for the chance to be reunited. She'd thrown fits and pulled far away from those who'd shown her kindness, preferring to be alone.

But now she'd met her cousin, and while she didn't know yet if that was a good thing, it was something different, at least. Something she didn't know existed before.

"Mrs. Hale said you didn't want to see me. I overheard her, in the hall, talking to Agnes."

"Well, she lied," Clement spat, his words sharp and bitter.

"Don't you like Mrs. Hale?"

"No, I don't *like* Mrs. Hale," Clement snapped. Her cousin laughed again, and then rolled to his side, curling up into a ball. "My mom died from complications only days after she had me, and I loved her so much, even as a tiny baby, that I became Living Gray. And then, late in the evening on the day that she died, Mrs. Hale showed up at our door. Starting then and ever since, she's taken my father away from me."

Lottie didn't understand how Mrs. Hale, who seemed to take her role supporting the family very seriously, could be to blame for keeping her uncle from his son, but she listened on.

"At first," Clement continued, "it was just little by little, pulling him away here, plotting with him there. But over time, she began to demand more and more of him, keeping him away for longer and longer stretches until I hardly saw him at all. He's grown so obsessed with his mission to find my mother that he's almost forgotten he has a son. Right under his roof. *Alive.*"

Lottie crossed her arms in front of her chest and bit her lower lip as a long-dormant warning roared to life.

Splintered magic lies.

It lies.

It lies.

It lies.

She forced it back, stuffing it away. She had just met her uncle and he was *helping* her, not lying to her.

"Don't you want to find your mother?" she asked, a bit more tentatively than she had asked her first question.

"Of *course*," Clement said. "But at what cost?"

Lottie shifted on her feet, uneasy. The feeling of being caught with her hand in the candy bowl before dinner crept up inside her—the type of twist in her gut that said she may have snatched at something far too quickly, without thinking through the consequences before she did it.

But twist or no twist, it was too late to do anything different now. What was done was done. She was already here. She had given up everything and placed every single ounce of hope on the idea that she'd find them. If splintered magic cost something, she had certainly paid her price.

She turned toward the items on Clement's dresser, and found a tall framed picture of a woman who looked so much like her own mother it nearly took her breath away. She stared hard at the photo. Her mother's eyes looked back at her from her aunt's face, and a deep hurt set itself inside Lottie's bones.

Yes. *This* was why she was here. To fix what had broken. To stop the pain.

"They looked alike . . . our mothers," she said.

Clement's thin lips formed the faintest hint of a smile. "In that case, you're doing a good job carrying on the family resemblance."

Lottie blinked back an onslaught of tears. If she could still blush, her cheeks would have flooded with red. People used to tell her she looked like her mother all the time. She hadn't realized how much she missed it.

"Do you cry because you miss her?" Lottie sniffed and wiped her eyes with the back of her hand.

"Sometimes. Whenever this cursed house groans forward, it reminds me of everything I've lost. Everything I'm still losing, even now, too, thanks to Mrs. Hale."

Lottie understood about crying. She had also cried a lot since turning gray. The grief and loss came in layers and waves. Sometimes even the smallest thing could set her off, like one day when she'd come in for lunch and couldn't find her mother's perfume. It turned out that Agnes had moved it when she was cleaning, but for the few minutes Lottie thought it was gone, she was a wreck. She had torn her room nearly to shreds trying to find it.

"She's only ever been nice to me." Lottie glanced at the door, thinking about the strange things Mrs. Hale said to Agnes in the hall, and wondering why she would have lied.

"Well, I've had more time with her than you have, and she's taken from me much more than she's given. Until we figure out why she said I didn't want to see you, I think it's best we keep our meeting a secret."

"Deal." It made sense, at least for now. Forsaken had a lot of secrets, and more and more by the second. Lottie got the feeling that she hadn't even come close to uncovering them all.

She pushed aside the growing stack of questions threatening to cast doubt onto Mrs. Hale's intentions. She didn't fully understand what the gray lady did, exactly, for her uncle, or why she made certain decisions, but she didn't quite want to give up on trusting that she had Lottie's best interests at heart.

But the truth was her uncle hadn't mentioned Clement at all when she met him, and that didn't sit right. If she knew one thing about parents, it was that they loved to talk about their children.

"Even if she did want to keep us apart," Lottie said,

"I'm glad I found you. I've never had the chance to talk with anyone my age who's like . . . this." Lottie gestured to herself. "In Vivelle, I was one of the youngest they'd seen that had turned Living Gray."

"Same. And that's coming from someone who turned gray as a baby." Clement bit his lip as if barely able to contain his own excitement at their secret meeting and their shared connection.

Lottie turned back to the photo of her aunt, then ran her gaze along the other items scattered around it. Things that would have fit in very nicely in the lady's room she had stumbled upon earlier. There was a pair of lace gloves, and a hairbrush. A long jewelry box with a rose painted over its curved lid. She lifted the lid, and a tiny ballerina rose from the box, twirling to a light, dainty song. The music player spun beneath her, its gears visible through a small glass enclosure.

When the song ended, Lottie pressed the lid shut.

"My mom was a dancer. Father once told me she danced to that song on her first night as the prima ballerina on Vivelle's Great Magician Stage." Clement gave a heavy sigh. "Back when he visited me more often. He said she had wanted to teach me to dance, too, just as soon as I could walk." He paused, a deep longing blanketing his face like a shroud. "But we never had the chance."

He forced a weary smile. "I have so many books about dance that she left behind, though I've been scared to look at them without her to teach me." He pulled a thick green book out from under the covers. "She also left me this story, and this one I read *all* the time."

Lottie gasped as she read the foiled words on the front cover.

The Enchanted Garden.

"There once was a door that wasn't a door . . ." she began, without thinking.

"And a bed that wasn't a bed." Clement's eyes lit up. "You know it."

"My mother used to read it to me, almost every night. But it made my suitcase too heavy to carry. I had to leave it." Lottie fought the urge to reach out and snatch the book from Clement so she could once again feel its weight in her arms.

"It's a beautiful story," Clement ran his fingers along the front cover. "I'm not surprised they got us each a copy."

"Yes, it must be very special." Lottie's breath hitched. She wondered if Clement knew that a strange, doorless garden was waiting outside, so very close.

"I've never seen you in the yard," she offered. "And I go out every day."

Clement snorted, like the answer was the most

obvious thing in the world. "You haven't seen me because I don't ever leave this room."

"Really? Why not?"

"Because this is where my father comes when he visits." Clement paused, looking as vulnerable as a cracked egg. His next words were shakier, and so much like a whisper that Lottie had to lean in to hear.

"I don't want to miss him."

Lottie's stomach sank as she imagined what it must feel like to be Clement. Waiting for days, weeks, months, years, for his father to pull himself away from the dead long enough to remember his living son. Being so desperate to not miss a single second that he had banished himself to his room.

Not so unlike herself, banishing herself to sit at the top of Forsaken's wall because of how much she missed her parents.

Lottie shuddered, then shrugged the chill off her shoulders.

At least she didn't have to worry about sitting on the wall as much now, because Henry Warwick would search the vastness of the In Between and find them. She had seen the steely determination in her uncle's eyes, and the smoldering splintered magic in his chest. He wouldn't give up until he succeeded.

And maybe both she and Clement could use a bit of change.

She spoke as gently as she could. "What if I told you I found a doorless garden, here? It reminded me of the riddle at the front of the book. I was trying to remember it earlier today, the part about the key so I could try to get in."

"Oh my." A flash of recognition crossed Clement's face. "Tell me—" He sat up and leaned forward, like a spark had ignited inside him and now zipped around, buzzing like a bee. "Is it at all like the story? With flowers bursting everywhere, spilling over the walls? Healing the entire world?"

"Not exactly." Lottie scrunched her eyebrows together. "But I could take you to see it. I could take you to see the doorless garden." She reached out to her cousin, an invisible thread from her heart to his. "Maybe we could try to find the door together."

The spark in Clement faded. His eyes darkened and he looked down at his bedsheets, pulling his lips to one side. "I don't know if I can, Lottie. What if I miss him?"

"Don't you think he'd find you? Do you think he'd give up on you entirely if you weren't waiting in your room?"

"Mrs. Hale said he's too busy to waste time looking

for things that aren't in their proper place." Clement's eyes met Lottie's in a cold, hard glare.

Mrs. Hale. Despite her hopes that Clement somehow misunderstood her, the gray lady was falling more and more out of favor with Lottie by the second. And she needed someone she trusted if she was going to survive in this place.

Which was even more reason why they *had* to do this. They had to at least try.

"What if we went, just for a little while? A half hour, an hour at most. Then you can come right back inside." Lottie held her breath as a wall of tension and silence built up between them.

"Okay," he finally said. "One trip. One time. But only because I know Mrs. Hale wouldn't like it."

Lottie exhaled, then grinned from cheek to cheek.

Things were looking up. Her uncle was using his magic to find her parents. She had a *cousin*. Whatever Clement's reasons for coming, they had a mystery to solve and a door to open.

And now they were in it together.

THIS KEY WITH THE HEART

Lottie ate a bigger breakfast than she had in ages. She stuffed biscuits and gravy, eggs and bacon, and a syrup-soaked pancake the size of her face into her mouth, barely taking time to chew before she swallowed.

"I'll tell my mother you've finally acquired a taste for her food," Agnes said with a wink.

Besides the abnormally large breakfast, Lottie made sure to act like this morning was otherwise *very* normal. She bundled up. She even took the staircase that would lead her out to the yard before waiting for Agnes's footsteps to fade. Then she snuck back upstairs.

She burst into Clement's room, where she found her cousin trying to button a pair of pants that obviously hadn't been worn since his last growth spurt. His sharp ankles poked out from under the hem like tiny mountains on his narrow legs.

Clement pinched his face together, a bit helpless.

Lottie stifled a giggle, then quieted herself and snuck, stealthy as she could, back through the closets in some of the abandoned rooms. She returned shortly with a long, thick coat.

"That's better," she said, once he had draped it over his shoulders and stuck his arms in the sleeves. It hung loosely over his thin frame, dusting the floor like a skirt. "At least you won't be cold."

Clement slipped on a pair of shoes that still fit, then stood. "Then we'd best get to it."

"Of course," Lottie said. She grabbed *The Enchanted Garden* off Clement's bed. "Let's go."

Lottie pushed open the door that would lead them outside, then made a break for the gardens, holding Clement's copy of the book tightly in her hands. But Clement didn't follow, leaving wintery winds to fill the space behind her where her cousin should have been. She turned to find him still in the doorway, shielding his eyes with his hands, hiding them from the light.

Lottie stopped and waited, keeping a watchful eye to ensure nobody was coming who wasn't meant to see them.

Clement removed his hands but kept his eyes pressed tightly shut. Then he opened them, slightly, slowly. He reminded Lottie of the newborn kittens she had stopped to watch in the alley behind their apartment on her way to an errand with Nellie in Vivelle. The creatures, tiny and damp, blinked at their strange new world in much the same way Clement did now. It must have been such a long time since he had even opened his curtains.

A few minutes passed, but once Clement had acclimated to the light, the two of them dashed across the yard. Lottie led the way, weaving through the maze of walled gardens until they arrived at the one without a door.

Clement leaned against the garden wall to catch his breath until the irritable ivy started wrapping itself around his wrists.

"What in the world?!" He slapped at it and tore off the tendrils that had grabbed hold of him, before backing away.

"It's like the whole garden's trying to hide," Lottie said.

"What's with all the hemlock sprigs around it?"

Lottie shrugged. "To keep out the ghosts?" She stared up at the wall and hugged the book tightly to her chest.

This time, she would find the key.

Clement joined Lottie as she knelt down and set the

book against the frozen-solid soil. She opened to the page with the riddle and read through the rest of the words she hadn't been able to remember before, noting that the wall really did look exactly like the illustration.

THERE ONCE WAS A DOOR THAT WASN'T A DOOR,
AND A BED THAT WASN'T A BED.
WHERE MOSSY GREEN CARPET SHOT UP FROM THE FLOOR,
THIS KEY WITH THE HEART MUST BE _____.

Her stomach sank. She should have paid more attention to the riddle back in Vivelle. She should have tried harder to ask the right questions so that now, when she needed it, she'd already have the answer.

"Have you ever seen a key with a heart anywhere in your house?"

"No." Clement shook his head. "Maybe *your* mother had it?"

Lottie thought it over for a moment. "If she did . . . it's gone." She blinked back tears, not fully understanding why this meant so much to her. But it absolutely *did*.

She wiped her runny nose on her sleeve.

"The key must be . . ." Clement continued. "I always thought the last word was 'red.' Because the line mentions a heart. And 'red' rhymes with 'bed.'"

"That's what I thought, too." Lottie traced her finger

across the blank. With her edition she'd assumed the exact same thing, when she'd given it any thought. It was the most straightforward answer.

But the only red thing she'd seen here was the cardinal, and he certainly hadn't helped her find the door. How were they supposed to find something red when nearly their entire worlds were gray?

Lottie sat back on her bottom. "Maybe the key is somewhere along the wall or something and it'll blend in if we can't see the red standing out from the stone. Maybe the Living Gray aren't allowed inside."

"That doesn't *feel* right, does it?" Clement asked as he sat back, too.

No. It didn't feel right. She and Clement both had a copy of this book from their mothers, and that had to mean something important. She couldn't imagine they would have given each of them the book only to have it lead to a dead end.

If the book was real. And if this was the right garden.

Clement scratched his head. "If we could find a key with a heart on it, maybe it wouldn't matter if we couldn't see the color?"

Lottie leaned forward and gave the riddle another, closer look, focusing this time not on the actual words before her, but on what the words *meant*. "What if the key is something different, like the carpet isn't really a carpet, it's grass . . ."

Clement gave a small smile, catching on to Lottie's thinking. "And if the bed isn't really a bed, then it can't be the kind you sleep in. So . . . what if it's a bed of flowers?"

Lottie's eyes lit up. "Yes!" she exclaimed. Maybe *now* they were asking the right questions.

"But I just don't see how any other word fits at the end of the riddle except for 'red.'"

"Right . . . but there are two ways to write the word 'red.' There's the color, and then there's 'read,' like *we read the book*. What if the key is the other kind, like we have to read it, somehow . . . with our hearts?" Lottie winced. It sounded silly even as she said it.

"If that's how you get in, I don't know that we'll be able to do it," Clement said after a brief pause. "We're Living Gray. Our magic is faded. It would take an awful lot of magic to unlock a door that isn't a door just by reading something."

Clement was right. Lottie fought against a wave of wanting to give up, to return to her familiar perch on the outer wall and pretend this never happened. But even though that seemed like it might be the easier, safer choice, she couldn't bring herself to quit.

"What if . . ." she started. "What if it isn't *our* magic

that will let us in . . . what if there's magic in the book, or even in the garden somehow? The Living Gray can still benefit from magic that exists in the world around us, even if it's not ours."

Clement paused, then turned to the wall with single-minded determination.

"Then we might as well try it."

"We should read it together, I think." They stood in front of the wall and Lottie held the book open between them. She imagined her mother and her aunt in this very place, many years ago. Maybe even with a tiny Lottie and a tiny Clement in their bellies. Holding the same book in their hands. Doing the same thing.

If they were right.

Lottie pushed back her doubts one final time and focused in on what she knew to be true. Their mothers had given them these books. This garden was without a door. And they might have figured out the key.

Clement wore a dreamlike expression, with his head tipped and his eyes fallen a bit unfocused. Maybe he was thinking of his mother, too. If that was the case, then it should be easy for them to read the completed riddle with both of their hearts.

"Are you ready?" she asked him.

"As I'll ever be," he said.

"There once was a door that wasn't a door," the two of them started.

The ivy on the walls rustled, barely, but it was enough for Lottie and Clement to exchange a quick glance.

"And a bed that wasn't a bed."

The ivy pulled away from the wall like a curtain and a warm wind whipped around the nearest corner, sending Lottie's hair swirling.

"It's working!" Clement yelled.

"Where mossy green carpet shot up from the floor."

A seam appeared around a large set of stones, and a bright, glowing light shone through the cracks. A high-pitched tone rang out, soft at first, then louder and louder until Lottie had to cover her ears. The book fell to the ground with a smack and the wind whipped again, sending a sweet, familiar scent past where the two of them stood. The scent of gardenia and vanilla. Their mothers' perfume.

"This key with the heart must be *read*!"

They nearly shouted the last line. The noise and the wind consumed them, and the glow on the wall grew and spread, filling in all the stones beneath and beside it.

Of course! The key with the heart wasn't red; it was *read*. They had needed to read the riddle aloud. *Together*. Lottie's heart swelled.

The wall's glow sent light searing so brightly into her and Clement's eyes that they had to turn away from it, no matter how much they wanted to see.

Lottie crouched near the earth and Clement crouched beside her, covering his ears, too.

Seconds passed, and slowly, the tone retreated. The wind stilled. Lottie opened her eyes and lowered her arms.

She and Clement stood and turned to face the garden wall.

Or, what *had* been a wall, only moments before.

THE GARDEN OF ICE
AND DECAY

A curved archway opened up to a wide view of what Lottie had seen through the hole in the wall the day prior: a garden that once might have been the most beautiful thing in the world, now encased in thick ice and drooping decay. The scent of old smoke that Lottie had noticed yesterday spread easier now that it could escape through an entire door.

Lottie lifted the book from the ground and tucked it under her arm. Clement reached out his hand.

She took it, and they stepped into the garden together.

Still and silent and frozen over, each and every blade of grass had been glazed with a clear coat of ice, like someone had painted them that way to hold them stiffly in place. An arched starch-white structure with broken columns stood crookedly to Lottie's left, choked by thick, black vines.

With each tender step they took, the frozen blades of grass cracked beneath their feet, leaving a trail of broken shards behind them.

The grass gave way to a curving stone path up ahead. As they walked it, they passed countless shrubs and flowers, shriveled and curled in on themselves like legs on a dead insect, and several crumbling statues, some with missing eyes or hands, or with heads fallen and split open. They passed a tiered fountain, with a stone statue of a woman mid-twirl at the top, her hands splayed delicately above her head. Her face tilted toward the clouds. Off her outstretched, pointed foot hung long icicles that hooked like gnarled toenails.

None of the statues in this garden moved.

They neared something attached to a barren branch of a small tree, almost like an abandoned beehive, with a small hole in the front. Lottie stepped up and peered inside. There she found a little mound of bugs with wings and dozens and dozens of soft, feather-like legs, all lost to the sleep of a long hibernation.

Lottie's mind flickered to the memory of a page in *The Enchanted Garden*, with an identical hive tucked in among the lush garden life.

She ran her hand along the book's leather spine and shot a glance at Clement. The look he gave back suggested he remembered the page in the story, too.

They continued on to where the path opened up to a wide lawn. At its center stood the blackened, sprawling tree she had seen from the top of Forsaken's outer wall. The scent of smoke grew stronger with each step, sending a sharp tang through the air as it emanated from the tree in waves.

Up close, the massive tree appeared not only dead from the inside out and encased with ice, but also from the outside in. Each branch was charred, like the bits of embers Lottie found in her hearth each morning. It was as if someone had slipped a coating of ice over the top of the tree while it burned, and the ice somehow kept it standing, preventing it from collapsing into a pile of ash.

Thick grooves ran up and down its wide trunk, and some of the topmost branches on the tree reached upward to the sky, while others toward the bottom dipped to the earth in the shape of a gentle U. A wooden swing hung from one of the branches on frozen lengths of rope.

Lottie paused and cracked *The Enchanted Garden* open, right to the center. A wide illustration spread across both pages, showcasing an identical tree, its sprawling branches thick with leaves. A swing, just like the one before them, hung from a branch in the picture, too. The illustration was gray now, but it had once been all deep greens and bright blues and rich browns.

Lottie's heart sunk at the devastating contrast between the two trees. "What happened to this place?" she whispered. Whatever it was, it had ushered in destruction.

Clement gave a start and pulled Lottie forward. He pointed, speechless, at an odd-shaped object next to the trunk. When Lottie realized what she was looking at, she gasped, too.

It was the strangest thing she had ever seen.

Shoots of root broke through the earth, though they weren't the sort of dirt-covered roots a person would expect from a normal tree in any normal sort of place. These roots shimmered silver and winked back at them, reflecting light from an unseen sun. They tied and tangled themselves together into the shape of a container with a flat lid.

There once was a garden that gave beautiful, magical gifts, and healed broken hearts.

Lottie could hear her mother's voice so clearly, she could have been standing right beside her.

Though she had sometimes wished it were real, she had always believed *The Enchanted Garden* was a lovely tale, but that it was *only* a story. Something beautiful and magical and once upon a time. But the door, the hive, this *tree*—Lottie's mother had to have known this garden was here when she gave Lottie the book. She must have known about it a long time ago, back when Forsaken wasn't Forsaken, and before Henry Warwick disappeared from Vivelle. When her sister was still alive. When the garden was alive, too.

She had told Lottie the story *so many* times. She had ensured the story of the garden had burrowed deeply inside Lottie's heart.

Lottie knelt to the earth and set the book down beside her.

In the story, the garden had given gifts that helped to heal broken hearts. And this silver-knotted box looked exactly like the kind of place a magical garden would keep its presents.

But clearly, something had gone very, *very* wrong along the way. She thought she had felt a pulse coming from the garden when she peeked in from outside, but now that she was here, everything was so broken, so frozen. So still.

No sign of life.

Breaking the heavy silence that had fallen between them since they stepped inside, Clement finally spoke.

"It's real, isn't it."

Lottie's mouth dried out like cotton and her heart took off racing like a wild horse. She managed a small nod.

"Do you think we should see what's inside it?" Clement asked with a slight waver. He knelt next to Lottie.

He had to know what this box might tell them if they opened the lid.

If they opened it and found nothing, they would know for certain that this garden was only a ghost of what it once had been. But if it had something in there for them . . . some kind of gift, it would mean that somehow, despite all the decay and ice . . . it was still *alive*.

It was almost enough to freeze Lottie there on the spot. She didn't know if she wanted to know the answer. Especially if the answer was bad.

But Lottie's locket warmed against her skin. She took it as a sign, pressed it to her chest, then let go and lifted the rooty lid.

It creaked like a yawn as it opened, like something long sleeping had finally stirred.

Inside the box rested a canvas satchel and a black pair of dancing shoes.

Clement snatched up the shoes while Lottie pulled out the satchel. Her hands shook as she reached inside it and removed a set of paints and brushes, a ream of thick paper, and a ball of twine. The items were all in shades of gray, at least to her eyes, which wasn't a surprise. What *was* a surprise, however, was how the tree knew she used to paint at all in the first place.

Lottie's memory sifted back to her paintings that once covered the hall. Her fingers itched. Without thinking, she ran them along the soft hair of a large brush. She stared at the paints, head spinning, as she tried to figure out how this tree in the middle of Forsaken in the middle of the In Between had known to give her this exact gift at this exact time. Had gifted back into her life something she had abandoned in her grief way back in Vivelle.

Her head spun so much, in fact, that she almost forgot about Clement, who held the shoes in his open palms like he cradled the world's most precious treasure in his hands.

"You're the only one I've ever told about the dancing," he said. But his face wasn't filled with wonder or even confusion like Lottie might have expected. It had fallen into sadness that quickly twisted into pain.

"Did you do this?" He backed away from Lottie, his eyes threatening tears.

"No, I'm just as surprised as you." Lottie stuffed the supplies back inside the satchel and stood.

"I . . . I need a moment." Clement dropped the shoes, leaving them to lie at odd angles on the ground. He scurried down the path and around the corner, leaving Lottie alone.

This was a lot for her—a girl who had lived in a city filled with people at every turn, and with endless things to do and see. It had to be even *more* for Clement, who only knew a life in the In Between, with its nearby ghosts and constant sorrow.

They needed time to figure out what this place meant for them both.

Lottie slung the satchel across her shoulder and stared hard at the tree, but when it became clear that it wasn't just going to up and tell her all its secrets, she walked to a nearby bench and sat down. She pulled out a single sheet of paper, a small selection of paints in different shades of gray, and a fine-tipped brush.

Then Lottie began to paint.

Simple yet soft strokes—of her mother's face, how it looked at night when her hair cascaded across her cheek as she sang Lottie a lullaby. Back in that precious, short-lived space when Lottie was old enough to remember and still young enough to be danced around the room.

At long last, the itching in Lottie's fingers grew quiet and the muscles in her hands relaxed as she gently held on to the paper. Somehow, here, even with a gray self and a gray set of paints in a frozen garden, she had still found a way to paint the *feeling* of the memory. The calm, the love, the drowsy, dreamy air.

Though her paintings used to do so much more than just feel like the scene they echoed. They used to *move*, too.

And then, right there in the garden of ice—a flickering more than a fluid movement—Lottie's painted mother swayed softly in front of the window and the little painted Lottie hummed along as she closed her eyes. The scent of her mother's perfume wrapped around real-life Lottie like a cozy blanket, letting the painted moonglow tag along. It spread out from the page and warmed her with its light.

Lottie glanced down to where her magic used to glow like melted gold.

A little golden flare winked back. Just a bit. Didn't it? A barely perceptible change in brightness?

No.

Lottie squeezed her eyes shut. She may have thought she saw something, maybe even *wished* to see it, but she knew it was impossible. She was the way she was because the light inside her had faded. Because her magic had slipped through her fingers like water. Because life was hard, and that fact caught up with her a bit earlier than it did for most.

She had imagined the painting moving, just as she had imagined that the magic inside herself was now a drop brighter. She wouldn't make that mistake again, imagining things that couldn't possibly be.

But no matter what Lottie did or didn't see, she couldn't ignore the fact that she felt a bit *better* after painting, and that would have to be enough. Since that terrible night, her sadness had tossed her about like a boat at sea during a wicked storm. Her feelings could swing this way and that within a single instant.

However, right now, she was watching the ocean roll with waves, but not from the deck of a boat. The sadness was still there, and it was still heavy. But in this moment, at least, she was watching from the shore, her feet planted on the sand, the water licking her toes.

Lottie didn't exactly know what to do with the painting, so she slid a bit of twine through a small hole in the top of the paper and walked over to the tree. Then she tied the picture to a low-hanging branch.

She let go just as a crawling sensation slithered up her spine, freezing her in place.

"Do you feel that?" she asked, hoping her question would reach Clement somewhere nearby.

No one answered.

"Clement?" Lottie turned one way, then another. She called out Clement's name again. Then a third time.

Her cousin wasn't here. Maybe it was too much for him, and he was waiting outside or had gone back to the house.

But the crawling feeling didn't go away.

Lottie had learned since arriving at Forsaken to trust her instincts, and right now, her instincts told her that someone was watching.

Just then the lunch bell rang, jangling over the top of the garden walls, making Lottie's heart skip a solid three beats.

She closed her eyes. When she opened them, the crawling feeling, wherever it had come from, was gone.

She tucked the satchel back in the box beside the tree, then at the last moment grabbed *The Enchanted Garden* and set it in the box, too. She followed the stone path to where it ended before continuing on to the frozen grass that would lead to the garden doorway.

But something was different.

Lottie couldn't quite pin it down at first, but something was different for sure.

And she realized—

Now, with each step Lottie took, the garden was

empty of the sound of shattering ice beneath her feet. It was empty of a trail of frozen shards behind her.

Somehow, now, in each place she set her steps, she left a path of melted footprints behind.

TIMMY

Lottie ate enough of her lunch to fill her stomach, and as soon as Agnes left, she snuck back down the hall. She would have preferred to *stomp* down the hall, but what with not actually wanting to be discovered, Lottie stomped in her heart instead of with her feet.

She threw open Clement's door and puffed out her chest, standing, as imposingly as she could at her age and size, in the middle of the doorframe.

Clement sat on the one small patch of exposed carpet with a tiny stack of books beside him, while pale light from the window streamed down in a narrow column across his face. Another book lay in front of his crossed legs, open to a page filled with black-and-white figures set in different poses. Each illustration had a slanted, curving note beneath it with a number and brief description.

Her cousin didn't even look up.

Lottie unpuffed herself and grimaced. She wanted

to scold Clement for leaving her out there alone without warning.

But, for some reason, she didn't. Instead, she sat down beside him on the floor.

"What are you doing?" she finally asked, bending her head low to try and catch her cousin's eye.

Clement kept his head down, his eyes locked on the open page. "These are the dance books I mentioned. My mom went to Vivelle's best school to study, and these were from her classes." He sighed. "I'm sorry I left but it . . . it was too much for me out there. I thought it would be fine, but it was too much. I just wanted to shut the door and return to the way things were before I knew what was out there."

Lottie couldn't exactly blame him. She understood what it was like to want to cling to the way things were before.

"But I also can't stop thinking about how the tree knew what it did. Like it knew . . . *me*."

"It knew me, too . . . I used to paint. A *lot*. And you told me your mother wanted you to learn to dance." In an instant, Lottie realized what the tree might be after. "Maybe the tree is telling you . . . telling *us*, that we still should."

Clement finally lifted his gaze from the page, his

face pinched tight in confusion. "But, how? *Why?*"

Lottie bit her bottom lip. She didn't have an answer, at least not yet. But using the gifts from the tree felt like the *right* next step to follow, even if she didn't fully understand it.

"I have a lot of questions, too," she said, shifting onto her knees. "I want to know why the garden is covered in ice. How it knew to give us those exact gifts. But I don't think we'll find the answers if we just stay inside this room." She paused. "One thing I do know is that our mothers loved us both very much. And if the garden is connected to them in any way at all, then it has to be *good*."

"Something good, coming from splintered magic?" Clement shook his head and turned away from the light. "I can't believe that, given everything I've seen."

Lottie still remembered her parents' warnings, but she hadn't been burned by splintered magic like Clement had. And the garden didn't seem turned or twisted like the rest of Forsaken.

"No," she said. "Maybe something good *despite* it."

"Despite it . . ." Clement inhaled deep and exhaled slow, as if steadying himself for something. "Then I'm taking these with me." He closed the book and added a couple of others to the pile, picked them up, and led the way through the door.

• • •

INSIDE THE GARDEN ONCE MORE, THEY HAD JUST ROUNDED the bend that opened up to the lawn when Lottie saw it.

The great tree stood a bit taller than it had that morning, and the branches reached a little higher.

But her *painting*—

She could hardly believe what she was seeing.

Lottie could count on two fingers the things she'd seen in color since she'd turned Living Gray: People who still had their magic, and the cardinal. That was it. But the picture she had created less than an hour ago, with various shades of gray paint, now hung in full color from its branch. A mixture of cream and midnight and honey— pigments so rich, so full. And she could *see* them. She could see them all.

The ice on the branch had melted, too, and droplets were still falling from it to the ground. Fresh grass was sprouting in each place the water had landed, forming small, bright green circles.

To top it all off, a set of fragile buds now popped out, dotting their way along the bark.

"It's melting . . . and it's *green*!" Clement shouted. He dropped his books and ran to the tree, cupping one of the buds tenderly in his hand. "What did you do?" he asked. "And how did you do it?!"

"I don't know. I just painted, using the present from

the tree. I painted a memory of me and my mother."

Clement's wide eyes took in all the change, all the fresh color. "But it looked *so* dead just a little while ago."

"I know." Lottie leaned in toward the branch and caught a whiff of springy sweetness. She couldn't help herself. She smiled, at whatever this was.

The change brought Lottie to wonder—no, not wonder. Something more thought-like than a wonder, but even tinier than that, and not fully grown. A thoughtling. With a hint of wish around its edges. Something that would be much too scary to hold on to as a real thought, or a real wish, because of the disappointment it would cause if it didn't come true.

Still, it was there, and it was this: If the tree could thaw, maybe the garden could heal. And if the garden could heal, maybe, just maybe, other things could, too.

But she didn't have much time to dwell, because the crawling feeling skittering up her spine from earlier that morning suddenly returned.

"Shh," Lottie whispered with a shiver, even though Clement wasn't talking. "Do you feel that?"

The look on Clement's face clearly said that he did *not.*

"Who's there?" Lottie did her best to sound brave.

She half hoped it was George or Agnes who had followed them in, and half feared it was Mrs. Hale.

When an unfamiliar silhouette slipped out from behind a barren shrub, Lottie yelped and stumbled backward.

"Please don't be scared!" A boy held out his hands and took a tiny step forward. "Oh, I didn't mean to scare you." He stuffed his hands in the pockets of his trousers, looking ashamed. "I shouldn't've snuck up."

Clement helped Lottie find her footing and the two of them gave a good, long stare at this new person, who continued his tentative approach.

This boy wasn't in color, like Agnes or George, but he wasn't exactly gray like herself or Clement, either. He was faded, like an old photograph or, better yet, like the wisp of a cloud almost disappeared from the sky.

On impulse, Lottie reached out to touch the boy's shoulder. It passed straight through him.

"You're a ghost!" she screamed, bracing herself against the tree trunk and grabbing on to Clement's hand.

"You aren't supposed to be here." Lottie was sure Clement had tried to sound brave, but his voice cracked on the last word, and he roughly cleared his throat.

"No—please. I mean, *yes*, I'm a ghost, but I am supposed to be here—I was invited!"

The ghost boy looked so pitiful that Lottie stuffed the next scream threatening to erupt back into her throat.

The boy gave a swift, airy whistle. In a flash, a bright red cardinal flitted over the top of the wall and landed on the ghost's shoulder, completely unaffected by his translucent state. The bird whistled and trilled and tipped his head to Lottie, like he was saying hello to an old friend.

Though still shaken, Lottie took the cardinal's presence here as a sign that this ghost wasn't anything, or anyone, to be afraid of.

"He wants to say hello." The boy smiled. "Seems like he might know you?"

"He does," Lottie said. "We've met."

"No wonder he looks so happy." The boy pet the bird's back with the tip of his finger.

"How did he get here?" Clement asked, turning up toward the flat, gray sky. "It's not like we're near a forest."

"That's a good question," the ghost boy said. "Before I was . . . like this, my sister used to tell me that cardinals were messengers from Ever After, to let those still in the Land of the Living know that their loved ones were all right. I always thought it was a nice tale. But I never found out if it was true."

Something about the story tugged at a memory, or the shadow of a memory, from when Lottie was very small. Yes. Her mother had told her about the cardinals being messengers once, while she held Lottie's hand on a spring stroll through the park. Lottie had spotted a cardinal in a tree, framed by bright green buds. Her mom had knelt down and whispered the story to her like it was some sort of exciting secret.

She had enjoyed hearing about it, much like she had enjoyed stories about fairies and other things that were fun to talk about but didn't really exist.

She wasn't sure she thought it was such a nice story now, especially with everything that had happened. Part of her wanted to hope that her parents would truly have the chance to send her some kind of a sign when they reached the mountains. But if the story was true, and if they really did send a cardinal, that would mean they were in Ever After. And she was counting on them being here, in the In Between, where she could still find them. It was the whole entire reason she came.

"I'm Timmy . . . by the way."

"Lottie," Lottie said.

"And Clement." Clement held out his hand, and Timmy looked at it with a vaguely amused expression until Clement caught himself and pulled it back in.

"Sorry," he said. "I've never actually met a ghost."

Timmy nodded, understanding.

"You don't have shoes." Lottie nodded to the boy's bare feet.

Timmy smiled. "Don't worry, Lottie. I'm not cold."

"Who invited you in?" Clement asked. "My father is searching the In Between for the people we've lost, but I've never heard of you."

"I used to live here once." Timmy looked toward the house. "A very long time ago, I think—time is strange when you're a ghost. I wasn't out there running for the mountains, or even moving slowly. When Hale found me, I was standing still."

"Mrs. Hale found you?!" Clement gave a quick glance at Lottie. "But why? What did she say?"

"Well, first she asked me why I wasn't moving. And I told her I wasn't sure I wanted to go to the mountains—so many of the ghosts act so *sure*. Like they somehow *know* Ever After is a good place. But I didn't know that. I don't know if it's good. Some people, and ghosts, have an easier time of it than others. It's hard for me to trust something that I've never seen for myself."

Lottie frowned. At least now she knew the difference between the ghosts who ran and the ones who stood still. Even if it was a bit of a sad reason.

"When Hale found me, she invited me in. My parents used to work here, back when I was alive. I knew the house, the gardens. I knew I'd be okay here. So I accepted her invitation."

"And you've been here ever since?"

Timmy nodded. "Hale's looking for my family. She said we could be reunited, and stay here at Forsaken, together. She said their name was on some . . . Ledger of Souls, so I must have been here long enough for them to pass away, too." Timmy's eyes darkened and his final words fell heavy out of his mouth, weighted down by so many years gone and memories missed.

"Then we've all got something in common," Clement said. "We're waiting for our loved ones to come back home."

"It seems like we do." Timmy bent down and peered at the thawed branch. "But this is remarkable," he said. "It started just a bit ago, right when you left, Lottie, and it's been dripping like this ever since. Reminds me of how the garden used to be, when I knew it, in the days it was first being planted. It was supposed to be a gift from Miss Dalia and Miss Elizabeth to their children."

Lottie's heart caught in her chest. "What did you say?"

"Right here, see?" Timmy led them around to the back of the trunk, to a carved heart containing their mothers' initials. "They were both expecting. Miss Elizabeth had an apartment downtown, and Miss Dalia had all this land and space at the edge of the city. Miss Elizabeth was gifted in—"

"Flowers. My mother was gifted in making living things grow, but she loved flowers best." A thick lump grew inside Lottie's throat. She surveyed the spread of frozen, wilted beds spread out in all directions and imagined her mother plotting out which plant would bloom in each one, with *her* in mind the whole time.

". . . Riiight," Timmy continued, his voice taking on a hint of suspicion, a grain of growing understanding.

"And Miss Dalia, my mother, was a dancer," Clement added. His chin lifted high but the wobble in his voice betrayed him. Maybe he was imagining his mother in this place, too, contributing her own special gifts.

"Yes," Timmy said. "She . . . your mother . . . gave the garden its rhythm, its movement, its song. But all that's fallen quiet now, too. I don't know how it ended up like this, though. It must have happened after I was gone."

The two Living Gray children and the one ghost fell silent, filled with thoughts of things lost and broken, faded and passed. Lottie's hands hung low at her sides, lonely from being so harshly left empty. Her legs buckled, tired from bearing the heavy load of sadness. Her heart thumped, slow in her chest.

"Our mothers made this garden," Lottie said, as she worked to assemble the full picture. "Which means our books were supposed to be companions to something bigger, not the whole thing itself. So we would know what they made for us, and what it all meant."

She continued, her words forming faster. "And if the garden is good, then maybe when your father's magic splintered . . . what if the ice *protected* the garden . . . saved it, somehow?"

Clement snatched up the dancing shoes from where he'd left them on the ground that morning, then took a step back, surveying the whole of the tree. A determined crease formed between his brows.

"If you're right," he said, "then I wonder if we can get more of it to thaw?"

The cardinal trilled, its song filling the air. And Lottie's own heart filled with something she hadn't felt in a very long time. Something that had drained out of her, leaving her dry and gray and empty, on a night when a stranger came knocking at the door.

She kept it tightly bound for a moment, too scared to release it. Then, with a deep breath and all the trust she could muster, Lottie let hope unfurl like a ribbon and float free. It twirled up into the frozen tree, then over the walls of the doorless garden, through all of Forsaken, and even outside it, to the In Between and beyond.

Because, if the story was true, then their mothers had made them a garden with the potential to heal the whole entire world.

By the time the dinner bell rang, Lottie and Clement and Timmy had laid out their plans. First thing in the morning, they would return with shovels, and rakes, and gloves for pulling frozen weeds. Lottie would add paintings to the tree, and Clement would work on teaching himself to dance as best he could.

If they were right, the ice on the tree would retreat and its bark would heal. In time, the thaw would spread to the lawn around it, then on to the rest of the garden. Then, even beyond that, maybe even fixing all the broken things, including the most broken thing of all. The thing that had come in the night and taken her parents from her in the first place.

Too scared to even utter the hope out loud and share it with her cousin, Lottie kept it secret and held it close to her heart.

On her way back inside, Lottie stopped and peeked around the corner of the garden wall nearest to the house. Agnes held the door open, waiting. Probably delighted that she hadn't seen Lottie scanning the In

Between for ghosts the whole entire day.

"I'll hang back and go up once the coast is clear," Clement said, leaning against a nearby wall, looking both tired and happy.

He caught Lottie's eye and a strange expression passed over his face. Something a bit amused, but also uncertain.

"Lottie . . ." he began, then stopped and shook his head. "Never mind." He smiled, then looked back up at the darkening sky. "Good night. See you in the morning."

"See you in the morning, Clement. Good night."

HOPE UNFURLING

The following morning Lottie sat down on the bench in the now-thawing garden and dipped a brush into a fresh jar of paint. Timmy hadn't shown himself to them yet, but Lottie felt him watching. Clement had found some pants that fit better, and now he tried on the dancing shoes for the first time, wiggling his toes against the stiff black leather. He stood and did a clumsy twirl before toppling over into the dirt.

She gave a hearty chuckle and, after a moment of recovery, Clement joined in.

"I don't know what we're doing," he said, pushing himself back up. "It feels silly. You really think that me learning to do this might mean something to anything at all or make any kind of difference?"

Lottie didn't know what they were doing either, really. "All I know is when I used the gift from the tree, part of it thawed. I think we need to trust that using the gifts will help."

As things stood now, they couldn't even pierce the frozen soil, not even with the sharpest shovel. While wafts of fresh air blew past them from time to time, the garden still glistened with ice and smelled like a recently put-out fire.

Clement twirled again and made a slightly sturdier landing, while Lottie put to paper another special memory. This time, of her father. It was a bright spring day, and she was six years old. The sun dappled light into their living room through the budding leaves on a tall tree outside.

Lottie had walked toward the window and tripped on a toy and fell. She cried out, and her father's thick, strong hands lifted her from the floor. His thumb rested on her cheek, catching a stream of salty tears. Her hiccupy cries slowed as he held her and her muscles relaxed as she folded into him.

She painted the safeness of her father. The strength. The easing of pain in the arms of someone who would always love her. Who had protected her then and so many times since.

After Lottie completed the final stroke, she set the brush down in a jar of water she had brought from the house. But she couldn't bring herself to look at what she'd created, at least not yet.

She carried the painting in front of her like an offering to the tree. She strung twine through the small hole in the top, then hung it from a branch next to her first picture.

A burst of aroma flooded Lottie's senses. Fresh cut grass, blooming petals, thawing soil, dandelion greens. She finally dared to peek, and this time, she saw it as it happened—as color soaked through the paper and spread like petals unfurling in the sun, overpowering the gray.

This memory was periwinkle and lilac mixed together with sweeps of springy green.

Lottie's magic *billowed* as her painted father's thumb stroked the little painted Lottie's cheek, as the leaves sent dancing shadows stretching across the sunlit room.

Clement pulled alongside Lottie. He took a sharp breath in, then spoke softly. "I've never seen something so beautiful come to life. We've got the crying lady in the hall, but she's nothing like *this*."

The tree shook in approval. Melted ice dripped from the branch where Lottie had hung the painting, splashing water onto the garden floor. The charred branch turned a deep brown, and little buds popped out all along the restored limb.

Astonished, Lottie finally pulled her gaze away from

the tree, its transformation complete. This garden had to have been built with some kind of powerful magic in order to withstand whatever had come at it the first time—the thing that left it looking like it did when she found it. And somehow the tree had managed to *keep* some of its magic, too, despite how many years it had been frozen. It was as if the magic of the tree was waking up from a long slumber, and that their presence here was helping to break the curse. As if the entire garden had been waiting, patiently, until the time came to start coming back to life.

Clement, too, carried a look of astonishment on his face, though he wasn't staring at the tree.

He was staring at her.

"Lottie," he said, his voice unsteady. "You're blushing."

"That's not possible," she snapped. "And it isn't nice for you to tease."

"I'm not teasing," Clement insisted. "If we had a mirror you could see it for yourself."

Lottie still didn't believe him, but she pressed her hands against her cheeks and even through her gloves she could feel it. *Warmth*. More warmth than she had felt since the moment her world turned gray.

But what Clement just told her was *impossible*. The Living Gray didn't just go around *un-graying*. Turning gray happened to most everyone over time, and once it did that was the way it was from then on out. Your magic faded. You grew up. Your sense of wonder got lost—or, in Lottie's case, snatched from her fingers one late fall night.

She dared to look down at her magic, just to prove Clement wrong.

But the glow inside her billowed again, this time enough that she could see it, leaving no room for even a shred of doubt. It whispered gently: *I am here. I'm still here.*

Lottie fell to the earth. She bent over her knees. A giant sob erupted from her shaking frame.

"No!" she cried out, squeezing her eyes shut and wiping a rough hand across them. The two branches she had thawed were barely budding. The hope contained inside them still so fragile. What if her tears caused everything to go back to the way it was? She couldn't do this here and make everything freeze all over again.

Lottie trembled from the pressure of the tears threatening to burst.

Clement knelt beside Lottie and set his hand on her back. "It's okay," he said. "You can let them out. The garden's survived far worse things than your crying."

Clement was right. It had survived something

horrible. But Lottie still didn't want to do anything, big or small, to hurt it.

Over the past couple of days, she'd discovered that impossible things were possible. And now she knew that something in this place had the potential to be stronger than all that had made and kept her gray. Maybe hope *could* rebound. Maybe faded magic *wasn't* the end of the story. She had seen it so many times in the Living Gray—a barely there glow. But she now understood that barely there didn't mean weakened forever. Or at least, not always.

Lottie's body shook even harder, and she gave in to the flood. Heavy teardrops fell from her eyes and splatted onto the soil. She knew the sorrow inside her tears would turn them into ice once they hit the garden floor. But she couldn't help it. She couldn't stop.

She let it all go.

Lottie cried for as long as she needed, let the things she knew jumble around and rearrange themselves while Clement knelt nearby, still and quiet. She felt Timmy's wavering presence manifest at her side, and the cool imprint of his ghostly hand on her shoulder.

Finally, Lottie opened her eyes, her vision blurry with blots and blobs from all the tears.

Her breath caught in her chest.

Because not even Lottie's blurred vision could stop her from seeing that *something* had happened. The grass hadn't frozen over, like she'd feared. Ice hadn't descended down the branches again. Instead, in the place where Lottie's tears had fallen, the frosted dirt had turned a rich umber, as if saturated by a heavy rain.

She blinked slowly then rocked back on her heels, trying to make sense of it.

Maybe, just like there were different kinds of flowers, and different people in the world, and different magics inside them, there were *also* different kinds of tears. Maybe there were tears that came from fear, or despair. She had cried those tears many times since that terrible, horrible night. And maybe those tears were even necessary sometimes—a natural thing that happened when a person lost something they deeply loved.

But the tears she cried now were different, Lottie was certain. These were tears that came from knowing the fullness and depth of what she had lost, and then realizing that there may be a bit of sun left to peek out from the dark, heavy clouds in her heart.

Grief and hope, side by side, mixed all together. And she knew from her father that hope and magic were tangled together in the most beautiful of knots.

Tears like that in a garden like this . . . The blur in

Lottie's eyes cleared and she looked down again at the ground beneath her feet.

Bunches and bunches of delicate blue flowers sprouted all around her, popping out of the soil and opening up in each place one of her tears fell.

"Forget-me-nots," Clement whispered.

"Forget-me-nots," Lottie echoed, her eyes wide and her heart open. Dozens of them popped out and bloomed, and a soft scent of warm wood and citrus and jasmine overpowered the stale smoke smell once and for all.

A whistle and a chirp sounded out. The cardinal swooped down into the garden and flew over Lottie's head.

Clement turned to the cardinal, and Lottie watched as a bright gleam of light passed through his dark, sad eyes. She could see it happening, she *knew* what it was, because the same thing had just happened to her.

For the very first time, Clement was choosing to believe that what he had seen happen to the tree—and to Lottie—might be possible for him, too. He stood and tried another twirl, this time fully sticking the landing.

"Did you ever see color return to anyone before, back when you lived in Vivelle?" he asked her, breathless.

"No," Lottie said. "There were more Living Gray than there were people in color, and Nellie always said this was just what happened to most people, in time.

Magic was seen as childish to some, if you held on to it for too long."

"Do you think it's childish, Lottie? Now that you know we might be able to get it back?"

Lottie thought for a moment, but only a moment, because her answer was as clear as anything she'd ever known.

"I never wanted to lose it in the first place."

Lottie walked over to her cousin and stood beside him. She reached a hand out to touch the newly thawed branch and its fragile green buds. They had already opened and were nearly ready to flower.

Timmy joined them, and the three children stood together.

Lottie imagined the garden filled with colorful flowers and magical plants, with healing weaving in and through everything and everyone inside it.

"Clement," Lottie said. "What if we can be so sad it hurts sometimes, but still also have a future?"

Clement took his cousin's hand and gave it a good squeeze.

And from the place where their feet met the earth, shoots of green burst forth, thawing the grass in every direction. Above them, ice turned to droplets of water and fell on the tops of their heads. More and more branches on the tree thawed and burst forth with tiny green buds. A narrow ray of sun slid through a thin place in the thick, heavy clouds, breaking the sky open and allowing a hint of blue to peek out from behind the gray.

And Lottie could see it.

THE THAWING

In the following days, Lottie and Clement dug their hands into freshly thawed soil. They marveled at grass stains on their palms. They stuck their noses in delicate lilac petals and inhaled their tender scent.

Their secret discovery took root in Lottie's soul, warming it against the chill of the gray. She was here, helping to heal her mother's garden while her uncle was out searching for her ghost. It had been more than a week since he left and Lottie last saw him, but soon, she was sure, they'd all be reunited, and she'd be able to show her mother and her aunt that their children had found the real enchanted garden and helped bring it back to life. They'd be so happy to see it, and so very proud. It would help them heal together.

A light wind carried Timmy's haunting whistle to Lottie's ears, giving her warning so she didn't startle when he popped up behind her. Turned out it was helpful having someone around who had been present for the garden's initial planting. Timmy knew a lot about what was what, and what was where.

"Those will be irises," he said, pointing to a small patch of green shoots. "And those will be gladiolus, and dragon daisies are coming back up over there!"

"I've never heard of dragon daisies." Lottie bent over to peer at the strange scaly stalks, only a few inches tall, with something red and orange pulsing from inside a tiny closed bloom at its tip.

Timmy chuckled. "You'll see, soon enough. They're one of my favorite magical flowers."

A low buzzing sounded out along the garden path, and Lottie followed it to the hive-like thing she had noticed on her first day here. Inside it, little now-yellow bugs had begun to stir. They yawned and stretched out their wings and wiggled their feathery legs.

"What are these?" Lottie yelled to Timmy. He joined her and peered inside the hive.

"Those are Tickles, of course!" he said. "Don't tell me you've never met a Tickle?!"

Clement joined them and smiled in at the waking creatures. One of the Tickles lifted up from the hive floor and flew out the opening. It landed on the top of Lottie's ear and danced on it with its little feather feet.

Lottie let out a giggle. Tickles actually *tickled*. It flew up and buzzed a twirl in front of her face before rejoining its friends in the hive.

All *this*, and it was only the beginning. Lottie couldn't wait to learn the rest of the magical garden's secrets.

If Lottie had kept time correctly, she'd left the Land of the Living four months ago now. It would be full on spring back in Vivelle. Fragrant lilacs would line walled gardens and tulips would lift their kisses toward the sun. She missed the seasons, more than she ever thought she would, especially now. But at least here, in the garden, they were building their own kind of spring. In fact, it was so warm inside the enchanted garden's walls that they threw off their thick coats the second they stepped through the archway, and remembered them only when it was time to head back through the wintery chill to the house, or when they needed to venture out to sneak gardening supplies from one of Forsaken's many sheds.

Lottie and Clement were both still mostly gray, but color had begun to warm Clement's cheeks, too, and the tone of his face filled in with hints of brown and blush.

Today, Clement had brought some of his mother's books on dance, and they rested haphazardly in a pile next to the tree. He lay on his stomach and held one in his hands, turning the pages slowly as he studied the drawings and diagrams. He kicked his feet up into the air behind him, growing more comfortable by the moment in his new shoes.

Melting droplets of ice plopped down on the top of his head, a favorite new game between him and the tree. Each time one hit him, Clement mussed his hair and smiled up at it. The tree shook its branches back at him, as if it delighted in having leaves once again that it could shake. The black, charred bark had begun falling off, shedding like a snake's old skin. Fresh brown bark now peeked through the places where the older had dropped and crumbled away.

A rhythm lifted up from somewhere deep inside the garden, maybe even from the tree itself. Invisible wind chimes. Leaves rustling in percussion. An aria of birdsong.

Inspired, Clement stood and tried some of the movements. He swayed to the garden's song, let it pull him under its spell. It wrapped around him as his muscles stretched, his fingers splayed, and his toes pointed. Soon, Clement added his own sweet, lilting melody, too. The gentle singing of a boy who'd known great sadness, with light echoes of missing and crescendos of hope.

Lottie paused her painting to watch him. His dancing

wasn't the same as a dancer who had studied for years under a teacher, but it was enchanting all the same. It was the dancing of a boy who had his heart first broken, then knotted tightly with despair, and who was now unraveling in the most beautiful way. Tears fell as he spun and sang, and in each place where a tear met the earth, delicate flowers sprouted and thin blooms unfurled.

The cardinal fluttered above Clement's head as he twirled and leapt, an unspoken choreography between them. Brown and red, boy and bird, dancer and song.

Timmy didn't show himself every day, but, though it didn't creep her out like it had the first few times, Lottie could often feel him watching.

She definitely felt him watching now.

She caught sight of him, barely a waver, kneeling next to a flower bed nearby. She left her cousin to his music and knelt next to the ghost, who stared sullenly at a bunch of crocuses robed in deep, royal violet. The dragon daisies had bloomed nearby, and now stood with tail-like stalks, and full-on wings, and a flower in the shape of a dragon's head. The tiny dragons blew puffs of smoke and flame from their little garden bed and roared and flapped their webbed wings.

"Are you okay?" Lottie asked, forgetting herself as she reached out to set her still-gray palm on his back.

It swiped right through him, sending a chill along her hand as it passed.

They rested in silence, watching a group of new stalks poke out from the soil.

"I don't know," Timmy said. "I always figured I'd been here a pretty long time since the rest of my family is in the In Between, too. But I've been doing the math . . . if you're twelve, that means I only died a bit more than twelve years ago, shortly before both of you were born. That means something terrible must have happened to my family if they're already gone, too."

Lottie didn't know what to say.

"I can still feel things . . . well, *emotions*, at least, even as a ghost. And today, I'm just sad." He gave a half-hearted smile, then changed the subject. "Hey—do you think you could do me a favor?"

"Of course." It was hard to see Timmy like this. She of all people knew how to spot sorrow. And Timmy was full to the brim with it right now.

"Can you run a finger along the petal of this crocus, right here? Describe what it feels like?"

"Sure." Lottie leaned forward and gently rubbed the purple petal between her finger and her thumb. "It's smooth, like dried wax on the side of a candle. And kind of like velvet if I rub it the other way."

"Yes," Timmy said. "That's exactly what I remember."

Lottie's heart ached at the missing that saturated each and every one of Timmy's words.

His face pinched together, conflicted and lost.

"When I turned gray, it filled me," Lottie said, her words pouring out quickly as she scrambled for some way to help him. "I was told I'd be stuck like that forever. I thought I'd better get used to it, that things would always be this way. To the people of Vivelle, letting your magic fade was just what happened to almost everyone eventually. I even tried to convince myself it was better, somehow, since I couldn't lose anything worse than what I'd already lost. But believing that didn't help anything. It just kept me focused on my sadness. I wasn't even open to the idea that I could heal—at least not like this. Finding my magic again. My color."

She paused and loosened up a bit of dirt with her fingers.

Timmy pulled his cap low, hiding his eyes.

"I'm just feeling pulled to my parents," he insisted. "It's not comfortable, but they must be that way." He pointed toward the mountains. "That's the direction I feel the pull. It's so strong, like a magnet. But we'll be reunited soon and then I'll feel better. Mrs. Hale promised I would."

Lottie looked in the direction Timmy said he felt the pull. A new thought drifted into her mind then, sitting so uncomfortably inside her that she almost didn't want to say it. Though it wouldn't do anyone any good at all if she kept it in. "What if the pull you're feeling isn't to your family, but to the mountains? To Ever After? What if you feel this way because you're supposed to let go and go there instead?"

Timmy scoffed. "A lot of good those words do for a girl who is *also* at Forsaken because she wants to find her dead parents and *live with them here*."

Lottie winced.

"Sorry. It's just . . . never mind, Lottie. I thought you'd understand."

Of *course* she understood. Mrs. Hale had made her the exact same promise. But at the time she agreed to it, Lottie had been sure that being together with her parents again, even as ghosts, was the only thing that might help her.

Now, she didn't know how she hoped it would all end up, but she knew her mom would be proud of what they were doing in the garden. And she also knew there were other things that could heal a person besides chasing ghosts.

The longer Lottie stayed and the more she learned

about Mrs. Hale, the less she trusted the gray lady. Mrs. Hale had *also* encouraged Warwick to search for Dalia without ceasing, so much that he nearly forgot about his son. And for some reason she had lied to Agnes and tried to keep Lottie and Clement apart.

But Hale had said it herself—she was grieving someone, too. And she had brought Lottie here so she could be reunited with her mom and dad. That counted for something, at least.

Lottie left Timmy where he was and returned to the picnic table. She pulled out a fresh piece of paper and painted her cousin, all thin, fluid strokes—more the impression of a boy than a technical portrait—with a tall tree, its branches and leaves like an umbrella over the top of his head, and little dots of flowers beneath his feet. Then, at the last moment, she added the figure of a wispy boy in a cap kneeling in the shadows, his gaze turned toward something just off the page.

THE NEXT MORNING, CLEMENT LAY ON HIS BACK AND kicked his legs up and down. Then he pressed his heels into the softened soil. He turned his torso back and forth from side to side, unable to contain the restless energy inside him.

Lottie's legs bounced, an energy building inside her,

too. She set down her paintbrush and tagged Clement, ready to start a fierce game of chase.

He leapt up and tagged Lottie back, then set off down the path.

Lottie gave him a moment's head start, stopping only briefly to inhale a new, particularly fragrant patch of flowers before darting after him again. Her stomach flipped and her arms pumped and her hair blew back behind her.

She hadn't played chase in so very long. And it felt *so good* to be back.

She caught up to Clement as he laughed and hopped from stone to stone across a small rivulet. He thrust out his arms, tipping them this way and that like the wings of a soaring bird until he had balanced himself on a single foot.

Clement shouted over the rush and bubble of the stream. "When everything is restored and back in full color again, including me, then maybe the garden will send its healing magic out to my father and tell him it's time to come home. And when he returns, the magic will lead him here straightaway. He'll find the garden door open. Then he'll walk down the path and see that the tree isn't burnt or frozen anymore. He'll find me beneath the tree, dancing, like my mother used to. And he'll know things are possible that he didn't ever before allow himself to dream."

Clement took off running again, but Lottie slowed once she hopped off the final stone. She had no doubt the garden's magic could spread as far and wide as it wanted, but she'd never in her life heard of splintered magic finding a way to recover. Those stories never had happy endings. Though she had also once believed that a person only had three choices: they could keep their magic and all their color; they could turn Living Gray and let their magic dim; or they splintered. She had been so sure that day at the train station that going with Mrs. Hale was the only thing that could help her. She had agreed to live here forever, to never return to Vivelle.

She knew differently now about the types of things that *could* happen and the types of things that helped. And if the Living Gray could actually heal, if they could regain their color and the magic they'd lost, then who was she to say that the splintered couldn't un-splinter, too?

ON THE WAY BACK TO THEIR ROOMS THAT EVENING, LOTTIE and Clement stopped in front of a long mirror at the end of a hall and took a good look at themselves. They could see the progress on each other outside, but here, with the mirror, they could see it on themselves.

Clement puffed out his chest and lifted his chin. His skin was still gray in splotches, but a warm brown in the places where his pigment had returned. His eyes had bits of amber speckled throughout, and his coat had cuffs of periwinkle and violet.

And Lottie was no longer a gray girl who would easily blend into the gray behind her. After spending so much time over so many days in the garden, she couldn't just melt into a wall anymore and fade away. Her fingers were still gray, and her stockings, and the tips of her hair. But there were also hints of flush in her cheeks, and strands of brown cascading from the top of her head in slight waves. The lace on her dress carried a hint of lime green. Her eyes were even deepening back to the color of chestnuts fallen from the trees.

And the golden glow of magic inside her chest—the thing that made her fingers itch to paint and that made her paintings come to life—was coming back, too, growing stronger and shinier by the day.

Nellie had been wrong. She didn't have to stay Living Gray forever. And it wasn't foolish to want to keep her magic and her color. Her road wouldn't be as easy as she once thought, but the work they were doing now was good, and brave.

Lottie stared at her reflection. She smiled, letting her

eyes crinkle at their outer edges, just like her father's. She imagined herself in full color, all the colors she was made of, a dazzling showcase of all that the gray had covered over. Already, color had pattered away at the sorrow, washing some of the layers off her body and her heart, letting bits and pieces of her true self peek back through.

But the peace of the moment was short-lived.

Lottie's heart summersaulted as a blot of pink shuffled into the mirror's reflection. The blot took a sharp breath in, then pressed her rosy lips together.

Agnes.

Lottie and Clement turned and pressed their backs against the frame.

"I thought I was seeing things," Agnes muttered as her eyes bulged nearly out of their sockets. "I thought, *Your eyes are playing tricks on you, Agnes. The shadows, the candlelight, they're making you see things that couldn't possibly be there.* But now, both of you here . . . and not entirely gray!" She wrung her hands together, then looked to Clement, her eyes pleading. "Hale told me you didn't want to meet your cousin."

"I didn't know I even had a cousin at all until Lottie showed up in my room."

Agnes swallowed. "I see. Oh my." She began pacing back and forth across the hall, still wringing her hands, deep creases of worry lining her face. "To start, and most important of all," she continued, "you can't let Hale see you like this. She's almost always wrapped up in her work for Warwick, so it won't be hard to avoid her. But make extra sure that if you need something you come to me, and that you run the other way if you hear her in the halls."

"Don't you think she'd be happy to know we're doing better?" Clement shot Lottie a look that said he already knew the answer.

"Well, I think it's *lovely*." Agnes stopped in front of the children, her expression both dead serious and a bit afraid. "But, no. I don't think she would."

"But why?" Lottie's face pinched together. "Why wouldn't she be happy to see us healing?"

Agnes's gaze lifted in the direction of the tower and her face fell.

Lottie's own stomach sunk as she, at last, understood.

The vat. The sorrow.

"The fuel." Lottie was still figuring out what ungraying fully meant. What she did know was that it was Mrs. Hale's *job* to help her uncle search the In Between for ghosts. Lottie also knew that she and Clement were healing. And the less gray they were, the less fuel they'd have. Less fuel meant Forsaken would groan less often, and the longer her uncle's search would take. In fact, she couldn't even recall how long it had been since it last lurched forward. And Henry Warwick had been searching for such a long time already.

Clement's brows furrowed. "This is *my* house, I should be able to do what I want to. Especially if it's a good thing."

"It is," Agnes reassured him. "But Hale won't see it that way, and while your father's gone, she's in charge of the house."

Clement kicked the air with an angry, pointed foot.

"We won't be able to keep it from her forever," Agnes continued. "But we can try to give you enough time to build a firm foundation before you have to face her, or until your father returns and you can show yourself to him. She can be fairly unpleasant when she's angry. And it's best, I think, at this early stage of healing, to be gentle on yourselves."

Lottie clenched her jaw and balled her fists tight, before forcing herself to relax and exhale. Even if Mrs. Hale didn't like it, and even if it did slow them down, she knew for certain that she didn't want to go back to the way she was before. A future filled with the cold, heavy emptiness of being fully Living Gray had lain before her like a nightmare that wouldn't let her wake up. She wouldn't go back to it if she didn't have to, she didn't think, not now that she knew things had the chance to change. Biding their time sounded like a good plan for now.

The jangling of Mrs. Hale's key ring echoing in a distant hall brought them all to a sudden silence. Agnes pointed at her head, a quiet reminder to be smart about their efforts. Lottie and Clement whispered a hushed good night before heading to their rooms.

In light of Agnes's revelation, Lottie fell into an uneasy sleep, but not before casting a wary gaze at the tapestries. The characters peeked out from various corners of their scenes, both tentative and curious. As if they just couldn't wait to see how things ended up, and what would happen next.

As time marched on in the In Between, Lottie, Clement, and Agnes worked well together to keep their secret, giving the cousins the space they needed to continue climbing out of the gray.

They visited the garden each and every morning. The statue at the top of the fountain, the one of the dancer, curtsied to them now as they passed. They settled in their usual spots under the tree and danced and sang and painted. They talked about happy things and sad things, the things they remembered and things that they missed. Each time they did, a shoot burst from the soil, or a flower opened, or a leaf turned its face to the sun.

The Tickles buzzed, and butterflies emerged from cocoons and flitted from flower to flower. The fountain itself thawed, spitting out water once again, tinkling like a cluster of bells. And the tree, now full with dark green leaves, shook off the final drops of water that had once been a glaze of ice. The columns and statues rebuilt their broken pieces and once again stood whole.

Lottie and Clement reread *The Enchanted Garden* in the enchanted garden itself with new eyes, discovering fresh magical elements tucked away here or hidden away there, all leaping off the pages of the story and spilling into the real world before them. Beautiful secrets planted by each of their mothers, just waiting to be found.

The air grew warmer and humid, like summer, and the scent of honeysuckle blew through on a light breeze. Smaller flowering trees rained down petals, and a world that was once so still and silent now moved, and breathed, and laughed and danced along with the children.

"Do you know what I want to do?" Clement said, as he leaned against the trunk of the tree. "One day I want to dance on the same stage as my mother. I want to *do* what my mother did. I'll train and practice as much as I can and for as long as it takes. Then, when I'm ready, one day

I'll bring joy to people through my dancing, just like her."

Lottie watched as the bright green magic flared in his chest.

She took in a slow, deep breath. Clement made it sound so simple. But whenever he talked like this, about what things might look like in the future, he never mentioned the other side of that coin. The side that said if he got to do that, then he couldn't be here. Clement spoke like he was ready to set off for the Land of the Living that very day if things worked out as he wished.

Even if they found a way around the splintered magic and could return, that didn't change the fact that ghosts couldn't cross back through the veil and into Vivelle. And right now, Lottie wasn't ready to let go of the hope that her uncle might still find them.

Though there was something else inside her, too, something recent and fresh—a sort of tugging in her heart. Like a magnet, as Timmy had said. Urging her to look forward. But whether forward meant Vivelle, or the In Between, or someplace else altogether, Lottie didn't know. At least not yet.

Whatever the answer, Lottie had now seen a burnt, frozen garden come back to life. She had seen flowers sprout up from tears, and color pour itself back into what had once been drained and gray. Who knew . . .

maybe her own future held possibilities she hadn't even yet begun to dream.

THAT AFTERNOON, CLEMENT'S VEINS DARKENED TO BLUE beneath his wrists and the buttons on his shirt deepened to indigo, the color of the Land of the Living's endless sea after a storm.

Clement laughed at the sight of it. He looked up at Lottie and grinned as the collar on her dress brightened to the deep yellow of the sun moments before it tucked itself into the horizon at the end of the day.

"How long do you think it'll take?" he asked.

"I don't know," Lottie said. "I think a very long time though, don't you? We became this way so quickly, but it can't work like that in both directions. I don't think it's something we're supposed to hurry."

"Agreed." Clement scanned the gardens, his magic pulsing brightly. "Sometimes I feel like if we could just get our color back and come out on the other side of this sadness, then everything would be easier because we'd know it all turned out okay. But maybe the point is we have to learn how to move forward without knowing all the answers. Maybe this isn't something that has any real sort of end."

"Like a rainbow," Lottie offered.

Clement exhaled a smile. "Exactly."

"It doesn't matter how long it takes." Lottie's magic flared in time with his. "What matters is that it's even possible at all."

THE FAMILY

A few days later, Lottie turned the soil around a set of flowers with thin mustard-yellow stems and transparent leaves speckled blue and orange and yellow, letting the oxygen in so the roots could breathe. *A Bunch of Bunches*, Timmy called them. Because they always grew together in a group. Their petals were made of something like stained glass, and were heavier than their stems, but as they grew in a bunch they overlapped and interlocked with each other, creating a system of support.

As Lottie stood to survey her work, a fleck of bright orange and yellow and blue caught her eye near the garden's outermost wall, like a piece of a puzzle fallen off a table and accidentally kicked across the floor.

She jogged over to it. Beneath a sprig of hemlock that poked over the top on the other side of the wall, in the ground right in front of her feet, a single Bunch shook under its own weight, fighting to stay standing.

The wind must have blown it over here when it was still just a seed. Without the others, its petals would fall, then shatter, and the Bunch would die. Lottie grabbed a shovel and dug carefully around its roots, then cupped the small plant inside her palms. She carried it over and tucked it in with the rest of its kind. It stopped shaking the moment it interlocked its petals with the ones beside it.

Lottie rubbed her dirty fingers against the fabric of her skirt and beamed down at the garden bed as the Bunch settled in with its companions. She was learning the garden well, and taking care of it well, too. As a result, now this fragile little flower had everything it needed to thrive.

She looked over at Clement dancing under the tree, and at Timmy, who had settled himself on the plush green grass to take a ghost-nap, whatever that was. He now lay still with his hat over his face. The three of them weren't unlike the Bunches in their own way, she thought with a smile. Everything good that had happened so far, they had managed to accomplish together.

Something still didn't sit right about the fact that Mrs. Hale had wanted to keep them apart, something that went deeper than the chance that they'd slow down her uncle's search. Though she didn't understand it just yet.

She shook off a sudden shiver, then rubbed the chill

from her arms and scanned the piles of garden tools they'd snatched from various sheds around Forsaken, searching for the watering can they'd been using for the baby plants. There were shovels, and rakes, and packets of seeds. But no watering can to be found.

"Clement!" Lottie shouted. "I'll be back in a minute!"

"Okay!" he yelled back, in the middle of an increasingly impressive arabesque.

Lottie bolted down the path. It was never an enjoyable errand, leaving the comfortable air of their garden for the unrelenting snowless winter of the rest of Forsaken, but she thought it might be a good idea to give the little Bunch a drink.

She zigged and zagged around corners, having long fallen familiar with the estate and its grounds.

Until she turned a corner and ran right into George.

George's sturdy, weather-worn hands caught Lottie and kept her from falling.

"Good to see you, Lottie," he said with a chuckle. "But where's your coat?! It's freezing." Lottie crossed her arms and rubbed her sleeves. The warmth of the garden had lingered with her well enough until now—until George brought up the actual weather.

The gardener's mouth fell open at the sight of Lottie's face.

"Agnes told me something was up. I couldn't bring myself to believe it until I'd seen you myself, but sure enough . . ."

"I'm not doing anything wrong." Lottie snuck a glance behind her. The garden's entrance was tucked safely out of sight around several bends and turns. And besides, they had a right to be there. The garden had been their mothers'—their mothers had *made* it for them.

George's eyes watered, and he ran his hand along the stubble on his chin. "Of course you aren't doing anything wrong. But it's cold out and you don't have a coat. How about you join my family for a warm snack before getting back to . . . whatever it is you're doing?"

Lottie breathed out a cloud that the frigid wind snatched away in half a second as it slapped against her cheek. A warm snack did sound nice.

SHE FOLLOWED GEORGE THROUGH THE GROUNDS TO THE very back of the estate. As she did, a drizzling rain started up. It sent bulbous drops splatting all around her, leaving her fingers chilled and her hair and shoulders damp.

She paused at what appeared, at first glance, to be just another door to just another garden. But this wall was built of warm red brick instead of larger, rectangular gray stones. The bricks were worn and rounded along the edges, and some were coated with a fine, fuzzy moss.

Agnes met George and Lottie right outside the door. She greeted Lottie with open arms, wrapping her inside a warm hug.

"Glad we'll have a chance to talk," Agnes whispered. "There are a lot of things we need to chat about and far too many ears inside that house." She pulled back and winked and gave a gentle bop to Lottie's nose.

George held the door open for them both. Lottie crossed into a tidy yard in front of a small cottage made of the same brick as the wall. Warm light poured from the cottage's square windows, and smoke spun out of a chimney that stood tall above a thatched roof. The smell of something delicious wafted from the cottage as well . . . warm, fluffy eggs and sizzling bacon.

The world outside the garden still appeared a bit faded, like an old photograph, to Lottie's un-graying eyes. But here everything was colorful and bright and smelled like something out of a fairy tale, before all the witches and wolves and evil royalty messed everything up.

The woman who must be Lydia, the one responsible for turning George's little garden into the best food she'd ever had, especially now that she'd grown an appetite to eat it, met them at the door. Her magic glowed the buttery brown of a bun fresh from the oven. Her dress hung awkwardly on her narrow frame, like she'd once better filled out the light yellow and blue gingham fabric. But her eyes sparkled, and her cheeks were rosy just like her daughter's.

"We're as happy as can be to have you visit, Lottie," she said. "Just happy as can be."

Inside the cottage, a glowing fire pumped heat into an open, cozy room that functioned as a living room, dining room, and kitchen. Two doors at the back of the room suggested bedrooms, and another door with a window led to a yard in the back of the house. Soft, well-loved quilts lay over the back of a wide chair, framed by worn pillows at each side.

The centerpiece of the room was a long wooden table, its surface covered in grooves and scratches. A chair at each end, two chairs on one side, and a bench on the other created a place meant for gathering together.

George stepped over to check on the food and Lydia ushered Lottie to the table, where she sat down on the bench. The place setting was simple: a napkin, a fork, and a knife, a white plate, and a glass filled with water. Steaming biscuits rested in a basket and in moments George brought over a skillet and scooped a hearty helping of eggs and bacon onto her plate.

This was definitely more breakfast than snack, but

even though Lottie hadn't met Lydia before now, she had built up a reputation for hearty portions.

"We eat a bit earlier or later than the rest of the house, depending," Lydia said. "Today it's late breakfast–early lunch. Hope you don't mind."

"It looks delicious." Lottie grabbed a biscuit and took a big first bite.

"Someone's appetite has certainly found its way home." Agnes's eyes glittered with teasing.

She was right, Lottie's appetite had come so far from her first day here. But she also didn't want to leave Clement and Timmy wondering where she was for too long when she had supposedly just gone to grab a watering can.

Turned out it was hard to quickly eat a biscuit that crumbled and melted like butter in her mouth. She wanted to savor it, to roll each bite around on her tongue.

"This is *delicious*!" Lottie said, not even caring that her mouth was still full.

Lydia blushed and took a seat at one end of the table. Agnes sat across from Lottie, and George sat at the other end once he had finished serving the others.

"Isn't this nice?" George said. "To have the table full. It's been such a long time."

The family nodded in agreement, savoring their first bites, too.

"Lydia's done all the cooking for the house for years and years," he continued. "That's how we met, a lifetime ago. She came up the drive her first day on the job pulling a cart of pots and pans behind her, taking in the sights with a cheeky smile and kind eyes. I was smitten from the start."

Lydia blushed again, her cheeks growing even pinker.

"Come on, you two," Agnes said, her voice playful. "Lottie isn't here for a mushy love story." She leaned in to Lottie, as if sharing a secret. "They do this much too often for my comfort."

Lottie finished off her first biscuit and then grabbed another.

"Agnes, I don't think you've tried a biscuit yet?" George asked, as he picked one up and lobbed it over the table at his daughter.

Agnes caught it with a laugh.

"And you, Lottie? Would you like some more?" Even though Lottie had clearly just grabbed a second, he tossed one up to her as well. She dropped her current biscuit and caught the new one between her palms. George winked and took another bite of his food.

This . . . this feeling of sitting at a table, as a family, framed by a playful father and a kind mother. It was familiar, like the summer dress she had once tried on after forgetting about it in the back of her closet for nearly a whole year. It had been one of her favorites and she hadn't wanted to believe that she'd outgrown it. She'd stretched it over her head and pulled it down over her torso, remembering the feel of the fabric, the softness of it, and why she had loved it so much.

But the truth was, she *had* outgrown it; when she'd tried the dress on again it had pinched her and squeezed her and made it hard for her to breathe.

Lottie had been working so hard to bring the garden to life again, longing to un-fade and reclaim her magic. Now, seeing a loving family all together brought that too-tight feeling right back. The empty, aching, endless missing of her parents and everything she'd lost along with them flared inside her, making her magic flicker like a candle on the verge of going out.

Looking at George and Agnes and Lydia all together was like looking at a reflection of the life she used to know. The life she was supposed to have.

"Excuse me." Lottie pushed the bench back from the table and stood.

"Are you okay, dear?" Lydia asked, her face a mix of confusion and pity.

The room that just minutes before had been warm and cozy turned suffocatingly hot. The air grew thick as syrup and heavy as lead. Sweat broke out along Lottie's brow and under her arms and on the back of her neck. Her lungs wouldn't open. She couldn't breathe.

Lottie gave a feeble nod. "I just need a minute. I need some air—"

She ran for the nearest door—the one that led to the back of the house. Once outside, she bent over, resting her hands on her knees. She sucked in the wintery air, her lungs filling quickly, hungrily. The drizzle cooled the heat on her skin.

She had come so far, but at this particular moment, the world made more sense out here than it did in there, with a family that wasn't hers, and a life she couldn't have. A life filled with color and magic *and* the people she loved beside her.

Lottie hadn't thought there would be people like them at Forsaken. And she couldn't pretend that it didn't bother her to see others whose lives were fine and good and easy from the start. The family inside that house didn't know what it was like to have your magic slip through your fingers, to be unable to stop it. All the work it took to even bring a bit of it back.

"It's not fair!" Lottie cried into the dreary morning. She clutched her stomach, fearing she might unravel like a ripped seam, or worse yet, crumble into pieces: bits of dust, and stone, and heartbreak the color of soot.

A roll of thunder sounded from the sky and the estate rumbled like an earthquake beneath her. Lottie imagined the levels rising in the vat in the room at the top of the tower as it leeched the sadness from her.

The thought didn't comfort her now as much as it had the first time she learned about the way her uncle was using her sadness, especially now that her healing was working against it.

"It isn't fair," Lottie repeated, her voice breaking. She let out the loneliness. The longing for the hands that weren't there to hold her, the arms that weren't there to hug her, and the memories she would never make.

Lottie didn't need a mirror to know that her hair had turned a bit grayer in the middle, and she could plainly see that her palms were now more ashen than pink. These were the kind of tears that felt like everything was unending night with no sign of day.

When she had cried herself empty, she stood and took a great, stuttering, steadying breath. Forsaken shuddered to a stop, having taken its portion from her.

Then something on the ground caught her eye.

In front of her lay a mound of dirt, the grass long grown over, marked with a little stone.

A grave.

The creak of a door sounded behind her—open, then closed.

"You're right, it isn't." Agnes's normally bubbly voice had taken on a quiet, somber air. "It isn't fair, what you've lost."

Agnes joined Lottie and they both stared at the mound.

"I need you to know something." Agnes pushed up her sleeves and held out her arms, revealing light colored skin dotted with patches of gray.

Lottie gasped. "But I thought—"

"I know you did," Agnes said. "Believe it or not, I was once completely Living Gray. My father and mother, too." She pulled her sleeves back down. "You can't know a person's whole life story just by the parts of them they let you see. And I didn't want to show you right away."

"But why not?" Lottie had come to understand that all the people she ever saw in color had never lost their magic or anything else. That they were like she used to be, with lucky lives. The friends her parents hosted for dinner. Her parents themselves. All the magic-filled people she passed on the street. She had thought they were in some special, unspoken club together. The ones with the easy road.

"Often, when grief is fresh it isn't helpful to tell

people that they'll heal, or at least have the chance to, somewhere along the way. You don't want anyone to feel like they need to hide how much they've lost, or bounce back by a certain time. At some point, though, you hope they'll be ready to start down that road. Sorrow, or despair at what we've lost, will still hang around, sometimes more, sometimes less, but we don't need to fear it. In time, we can find room once more for joy, and laughter, and peace. Un-fading isn't a fast process, and it isn't a straight line."

Lottie pulled her lips to the side and thought about what Agnes said.

When she first arrived at Forsaken, she'd just lost her parents. Just given up a life in Vivelle because of that. If someone had told her she could one day feel better, even a little, and *especially* without getting them back, she wouldn't have wanted to hear it.

What Agnes showed her now . . . it changed the lens of so much of what Lottie had thought to be true. It also gave an important answer to something she hadn't understood since the moment she found out about this side of her family. Her mother and her aunt—they had loved each other very much; the garden, their shared project, was plenty proof of that. But her mom had been so full of life and love and laughter. If a person could become Living Gray and slowly heal in time, maybe her mom *had* faded when Dalia died. Lottie was so small; she wouldn't have remembered.

There were *so many* Living Gray in Vivelle. Either most of them didn't know it was possible to regain their magic and color, or they didn't trust it. The way people talked, especially people like Nellie, even if they did know, maybe they thought it was safer to just stay gray.

But now that Lottie knew at least *some* others had done what she was doing, she would never assume to know someone's story just by looking at them again.

Lottie approached the mound and knelt on the grass beside it when her gaze caught on something tucked away behind the stone. No, *two* things, both ragged and worn from exposure, made of leather, with dirty long cords lacing up the front of each.

A pair of shoes.

"Those shoes belonged to my brother." Agnes knelt as well and ran a hand along the top of the cracked leather.

"I was six," she continued with a sad smile. "He was twelve. My parents had wanted many, many children, but they got the two of us. He was a strong boy, who ran in and out of the gardens, who befriended the birds. As a nod to the running joke in the family we put these here, in case he finally needed them on his way to Ever After. Because, while he was alive, unless my parents made him, he never wore shoes."

Lottie's throat went dry. She thought of the only boy she'd ever met who never wore shoes.

Don't worry, Lottie, I'm not cold.

Lottie stumbled back from the grave.

"What is it?" Agnes reached out her hand. "Are you okay?"

No, Lottie wasn't okay. Nothing about this was okay.

"He's been so sad," Lottie whispered. "He's been so sad for such a long time."

"Who's sad, Lottie?" Agnes's voice took on a desperate edge, and a pallor fell across her face. "Please, tell me who is sad?!"

It didn't make any sense that a ghost boy in a doorless garden was waiting for his family to join him from the In Between for years, while they had been right outside the garden walls, very much still alive, the whole entire time.

"Timmy." Lottie's entire body shook as one fear-filled gaze met another. "He's here."

HEMLOCK

Lottie led George, Agnes, and Lydia into the garden and down the path. Timmy had woken from his nap and now sat, staring off, like he did more and more often these days, at the mountains.

"Oh." Lydia covered her hand with her mouth. She sprinted to him, and Timmy turned just in time to feel her open arms grasping empty air. Then she cried as Timmy drew near, in the closest thing they could get to a hug.

George and Agnes approached more slowly. They held out their hands, touching their skin to the wisp that was Timmy as he hugged his mother.

He pulled away and failed to blink back tears as he looked at each member of his family. "But you aren't—" Timmy started. "Hale said—"

"Mrs. Hale told him you'd be ghosts. That you were in the In Between, like him," Lottie explained.

A stunned-silent Clement joined her near the family.

George, Lydia, and Agnes exchanged worried glances with one another.

Timmy took a shaky, ghostly breath. "I don't understand. She said she'd find you, like she found me, and then we could be together. I've been waiting. I thought we would be . . . the same."

"We've been here the whole time, son," George said, his own face pulled tight in pain. "When we lost you, we buried you behind the house and continued working for Warwick. When his magic splintered, we stayed. At first, we agreed to come along so we could find you. He and Hale spoke like that was the only way out of the sadness. But in time, we found there were other ways, too. At some point along the way, as the years went by, we stopped asking if he'd found you. And we tried to accept the fact that you might really be gone."

Timmy turned away and pulled his hat down over his eyes.

"Not because we didn't miss you!" George continued, his voice verging on desperate. "And not because we forgot, not even a little bit. The only reason we're here at all was because we lost you not long before Henry lost his wife. When he told us what he was doing, we thought his splinter meant we'd have a chance to be with you a while longer.

"So we made our choice, and stayed on to help with the estate. But coming here—following Warwick through the In Between—did nothing to free us. It did *nothing* to help. We're trapped in a place that wasn't meant for the living. We've done our best to heal *despite* it. And the last thing we wanted to do was keep you trapped here with us, too. It's called the In Between for a reason. We don't belong here yet, and you don't belong here forever. It's merely a road you're meant to take on the way to somewhere else."

"But *why?*" Timmy yanked off his hat and let it fall to the earth. He looked up at his father with a drawn-open mouth and a quivering chin. "Why didn't she tell you she found me?"

Lottie stepped backward until she felt the great tree's thick roots poke out of the ground beneath her. She closed her eyes and rested her head against the bark. She let the magic of it pulse through her while she fought to stay calm.

Agnes, and Lydia, and George now had what she herself had wanted so badly since the night she turned gray, the night she offered to bargain her magic for her parents. They were now reunited with the one they had lost.

And though she couldn't put her finger on it, something wasn't right.

Timmy wasn't happy here. She'd been around him long enough to understand that. He'd blamed it on feeling pulled in the direction where he thought his family was—but they had been right outside the garden this entire time. Which meant that Lottie had been right. The pull Timmy was feeling must have been toward Ever After—not toward his loved ones. Because that's where he was meant to go.

Lottie thought back to that wretched night and the weeks that followed her parents' deaths. When she'd thought that finding their ghosts was the only thing that could help her possibly survive. But Agnes and her parents had found a way to heal long before now, *without* being reunited.

She had thought at first that if they healed the garden, it would have the power to heal all the broken things. And that healing what had broken meant that it would help her get her parents back. But she and Clement, without being reunited with the ones they had lost, had started to heal, too.

Lottie opened her eyes as she realized that maybe the garden's healing power had less to do with bringing her parents back to her, or taking away all the bad and broken things in the world, and more to do with healing the wounds inside her own heart.

And beyond that, if George was right—that the In Between was only ever meant to be a temporary place, and that it wasn't any more natural for Timmy to linger here forever than it was for living people to be here at all—what did that mean for Lottie? For all of them?

They had all made the same bargain. Each living person here had agreed to come in exchange for the chance to live in the Land of the Dead and chase after ghosts. Even if they didn't want to be here anymore, they couldn't go back. That was the deal.

Splintered magic had enticed them, and it was too late to make a different decision. The permanence of it crushed Lottie's heart like it was a ball of paper. They were no better than insects trapped in a web. They could wiggle all they wanted, but the web just choked them tighter and tighter as they tried.

Worse still, they didn't know what Warwick would do when he returned and learned that the source of fuel for his mission had been so much depleted. Or, even if he wasn't angry about that, whether he would, or if he even *could*, find a way to bring them back where they belonged.

But they weren't the only ones who couldn't leave.

"Timmy." Lottie interrupted the family's scattered, spotty attempts to sort out what had happened and how they might be able to fix it. "You said Hale brought you here. How exactly did you get into this specific garden?"

"Hale invited me into Forsaken." Timmy blinked. "I was so excited to be someplace familiar again that I ran around all the gardens for what felt like hours at the time. Hale followed behind me, smiling and encouraging me to go on. I could tell right away that things had changed. The color was gone. I had heard about splintered magic, but my return to Forsaken was the first time I'd seen its effects for myself. The splinter had cracked things, and made things rot and die that used to be so lively, but there was still so much here, hiding beneath all that, that felt like home.

"Hale seemed so glad that I had been found, so hopeful that it was a *good* thing. After a while, she reminded me of this garden and suggested I find it. It had been the most beautiful place in the world, at least at the time I left it, so of course I ran to see it as fast as I could. I didn't remember the riddle to get inside, but as a ghost I could go through walls. She gave me permission to go in without her." He paused, and his words slowed. "But when I wanted to leave, I couldn't get back through . . . Time got kind of blurry after that, but it must have been years. And then you came, and Clement."

A small spiral of horror kicked up inside Lottie,

something tighter and wilder than the gentle cyclone that had spun in the air in Vivelle on her last night with her parents. She kicked herself for not having seen it before. Her father would have seen it, he would have seen the misplaced piece right away. The thing that didn't fit. She'd been so caught up in her own sorrow, and then in her own healing, she'd missed the bigger picture.

"Come with me," Lottie said. "I don't know why she kept you stuck here, Timmy, but I do know how." She bolted down the path, and the rest followed behind. Timmy lingered, trapped behind the curved archway, while Lottie ran out and motioned for everyone else to join her on the other side.

She glared at the hemlock lining the garden's walls.

"Hale told me that these hemlock sprigs keep the ghosts out who haven't received an invitation. But they're not only lining Forsaken's outer wall, they're lining this *entire garden*, too. Which means that hemlock doesn't just keep ghosts out. It also keeps them locked *in.*"

Lottie looked at Timmy, at the pain on his face as the reality of her words settled in.

"She had me *grow* this hemlock for her." George snatched the nearest sprig off the wall and crumpled it between his fists. "I knew she'd put some in here but I didn't know why. I thought this garden had burned up, that it had been destroyed when Warwick's magic splintered."

"It was," Clement said. "Well, nearly. When we found it, it was burned, but also covered in ice."

"We've been lied to," Agnes said, her words carrying a sharp, angry edge for the very first time.

Yes. Lottie's own stomach billowed a flame that hadn't reared its fiery head in a long, long while. Not since that day in the hall when she'd heard Clement crying.

Mrs. Hale had lied to them all.

Lottie turned to the house just as a light flickered on in the tower.

THE SPLINTER

"It should be me," George said, casting a nervous glance at the warm light coming from the topmost part of the estate. "I've known him the longest."

"Well, it's certainly not going to be me," Timmy deadpanned. "Unless you all want to spend the next few hours removing my enchanted hemlock cage."

"No," Lottie said, surprising even herself at her confidence. "I'll go. George, Lydia, Agnes, you can start to remove the hemlock."

Lydia and Agnes and even Timmy smiled. He looked up at the wall with defiance and swung his fist at the air.

Lottie would tell her uncle what Hale had done and hope that even through his splintered magic he'd find a way to make things right.

She turned to her cousin.

"You said you wanted your father to see you dancing beneath the tree. You said when he does, he'll know things are possible that he never even dreamed. For any of this to be made right, we're going to need him to do more than know it, we need him to believe it for himself, too."

Clement nodded, and they both faced the tower.

The old Lottie would have run straight up to the very top to ask her uncle if he'd found her parents, but there were different things at stake now. Things that had much more to do with her own life and her chance to fully live it than to do with chasing ghosts.

"I'm going up there, and I'm going to bring him back here." She reached out for her cousin's hand and held on to it tightly. "It's time to bring him to the garden."

The whole way into the house and up the stairs, Lottie rehearsed what she'd say to her uncle. How she'd break it to him that Mrs. Hale, the angel who appeared on his doorstep the day he lost his wife, had done something awful. She was ready for the sight of his smoldering magic and severe angles and deep-set eyes. For the disappointment to fall over his face, for his shoulders to slump, even for him to insist that there had to be some kind of misunderstanding.

What she wasn't ready for was reaching the top of the tower and not finding Henry Warwick at all.

Instead, she found Mrs. Hale.

Lottie reached her hands up to hide her face by instinct, but quickly lowered them, because it wouldn't make any difference. After a long while avoiding Mrs. Hale at all costs, for better or worse, her secret was about to be revealed.

And she was too mad to be afraid.

The gray lady, the one whose magic had gone completely out, bent over the Ledger of Souls, her silver face a mix of harsh light and deep, crater-like shadows.

Mrs. Hale looked up at Lottie, then sighed.

"Oh, Lottie," she said, her voice flat as a piece of paper. "What have you done."

"What have *I* done?!" Lottie clenched her fists in frustration. "I came here to see my uncle. Where is he?"

"Henry isn't here." Mrs. Hale pulled out her clock and raised a single brow as she peeked at the time. "I'm afraid it's only me." Then she painted on a condescending smile. "But at least in seeing you, I've answered a very pressing question. Follow me, Lottie."

Lottie humphed, but she stomped after the woman. Without her uncle, she had to recalculate. She either had to confront Mrs. Hale and force her to make things right, or find a way to somehow fix things in spite of her.

Mrs. Hale led Lottie to the room off to the side of the

stairs. The one with the gears, and the high lever, and the vat of oily sorrow—which now sat less than half full.

Lottie's heart soared at the sight. She knew that she and Clement were healing. She could see it on their bodies and feel it in her heart. But here was another visible sign. There wasn't as much sorrow to leech from them as there had been before.

Hale gestured to the vat. "I think we've found our problem, don't you?"

Lottie narrowed her eyes. She knew Mrs. Hale would see things differently, but less sorrow in the vat meant that *good* things were happening. Not bad.

"I don't see any problem."

"Very well, if I must spell it out," Mrs. Hale spat. "We can't find your parents if we can't move. At the moment, we're using more than we're taking in. And for some reason, your uncle's on his way here right this moment without having found any ghosts, though he should have still had enough supplies to last several more weeks."

Lottie smiled as she thought about what Clement had said a while back. Maybe the magic of the garden had somehow really reached out to her uncle and called him back home.

"I wouldn't smile if I were you, child. He'll be here *very* soon. And he'll be *so* disappointed when he returns.

Have you seen splintered magic when it's angry, Lottie? It isn't a pretty sight."

For some reason, despite Mrs. Hale's warning, Lottie didn't feel afraid. She imagined Henry Warwick, out there, wandering the In Between, the wind whipping across his cheeks as he searched each ghostly face for the hint of someone familiar. She had thought he was so full of power when she met him, that his smoldering magic was fearsome to behold. She had been so focused on her own sorrow, and on his promise that he would help her, that she didn't realize he was caught in the web of splintered magic, too. To go on like that, for *years,* without sleeping, without stopping. Only taking in the smallest amount of food and water to keep himself alive. Even when his eyes sunk back and his bones poked out at sharp angles beneath papery skin.

And on top of it all, he literally fed off people's sadness in order to do it.

Her uncle wasn't free. He wasn't powerful. He was broken, just like her.

"Don't you feel tired, Lottie?" Mrs. Hale asked, her voice taking on a softer, more inviting tone. Just like it had that day at the train station, when she had tricked Lottie into leaving everything behind. "Don't you realize that losing your parents is only the first of your great sorrows? You'll lose the only other people you have as well. You'll be denied things you want badly. You'll have to fight the gray and the fading again, and again, and *again*. Even if you aren't now, you'll get tired of fighting. Most everyone does, even when surrounded by the lights and colors of Vivelle."

Lottie hurt as she thought of Nellie, who had said such similar things. For her and so many others, being Living Gray seemed like the safer choice. Her magic faded, but she also felt buffered from pain. Lottie had understood it well herself on the day Nellie had tried to get her to paint, shortly after she lost her parents. She had taken strange comfort in the fact that a person's hopes couldn't be crushed if they didn't have any hopes to start with. Their heart couldn't break again and again if they never picked its pieces up off the floor.

Lottie pressed her locket close to her chest. Her parents didn't know they would leave her so soon, and Lottie was sure there were so many more things they had planned to teach her. But they believed in her gift and her magic. They wouldn't want her to despair, at least not forever, and especially not now that she felt ready to try to heal.

"You're right," Lottie said, her words slow and even to start. "I might face a hundred hard things in my life or more, all enough to turn me Living Gray. And each time I might have to fight to keep my magic glowing strong. But I don't care." She spoke a bit bolder as she continued. "I don't care how many times I have to fight." Then she paused, and let go of the locket, letting its warmth seep through her skin. "Life doesn't have to be easy to still be *good.*"

Mrs. Hale pressed her lips together, unamused. She tipped her head to the side like an impatient adult looks at a toddler who refuses to quit babbling about the duck they saw at the park, or their squeaky new pair of shoes.

"And besides"—Lottie pulled her shoulders back and lifted her chin—"I wouldn't expect you to understand. You enjoy tricking people who've lost everything. You try to make them sadder. You try to make things *worse.*"

"Oh, really?!" Hale said in mock surprise. Then her tone turned biting. "In that case, you should be angry at your uncle. I'm only doing the work Warwick has *asked* me to do."

Lottie pushed against Hale's attempt to distract her by deflecting the blame. Even if it was her uncle telling her to do it, Hale still had chosen to harvest sorrow from so many people Lottie had grown to love, for so very many years. She wouldn't fall for any more of Hale's deception.

She looked the gray lady straight in the eyes. "I found Timmy."

Hale breathed in sharply, then her lips pulled into a sneer. "Almost forgot about him." She tilted her head even further, at an almost unnatural angle. She blinked once, then *laughed*, something cackling and grating, like a ripping seam.

"How could you forget him?!" Lottie yelled as the echoes of Hale's laughter faded. "You left him trapped. He thought his family was dead and that you were working with Warwick to reunite them. He's been waiting there, all this time, *alone*."

Hale shrugged and turned to tend to the huge machine, adjusting its levels with expert precision. "I selected people for this journey for *very* specific reasons, Lottie. Practical ones, who'll grow things and cook things and clean things for the house. But also, people who'll help us *get* where we need to *go*. About a year into our journey, when Timmy's *family* decided that they wanted to un-gray themselves, we ran short on fuel, and thus we had a problem. You hadn't yet arrived, gracing us with all that thick sorrow oozing out of you, seeping out your pores, weighing down the air with your sadness. So I sought the boy's ghost and invited him in to make up the difference. Ghosts can be an *excellent* source of sorrow, if you pick the right ones."

She tweaked another control, then turned briefly back to Lottie. "They're together now, I presume?"

Lottie didn't answer.

"Then it's settled. Though keeping people apart is often a delicious component of growing sorrow to harvest, the family's been reunited, and I've fulfilled my promise." Her voice took on an edge of ice. "I always do."

Nothing Hale said sat right. None of it felt good. She had once and for all dropped the kind and comforting airs she'd put on back when they first met. This woman here was cold, and calculating, and single-minded. Too busy tweaking the machine to even listen, or pretend to care. No wonder Agnes had known Mrs. Hale wouldn't like them regaining their color. She'd hated when Agnes and her parents had first done it themselves.

And she'd planned to help keep Lottie and Clement sad by keeping them apart.

The last thing Hale had said churned especially sour in Lottie's stomach. "But they aren't together like they're meant to be. He's a ghost and they're alive. It isn't natural. You told him they'd be the same."

Hale smirked. "Says the living girl who gave up everything to live with her own ghost parents."

"That's not fair." Lottie cringed. "I didn't see any

other way. I couldn't. Not when I was that sad and you had just told me I could get them back."

Lottie thought back to that day at the train station, when she agreed to follow her uncle's splintered magic across the veil. When Mrs. Hale told Lottie that never being able to return was the price to live with them in the In Between forever. It had sounded *so good* at the time.

Timmy's family had agreed to it, too, back when they'd been drowning in their own grief. And her uncle had led the charge, and been out here ever since shortly after his magic splintered.

They had all made the exact same deal. The chance to be reunited. The price: never being able to leave. But Mrs. Hale, who said she'd lost someone too, *had* left. She had left Forsaken to find Timmy, and to pick up Lottie in the Land of the Living.

Lottie had stuffed her father's warnings about the Stone Man and splintered magic deep down and far away. It had been the only way she could come here: if she chose to believe that her uncle had found a way to use his splinter for good. But her father had been right all along when he taught her there were always repercussions to splintered magic. There was always a catch.

And Hale hadn't been helping anyone. She'd been using them all.

She had been the one to invite Timmy. And bringing Lottie to Forsaken had been *her* idea as well. Hale had shown up on the doorstep the day Warwick's magic splintered. She arrived with a broom and a plan, he had said. But something about the scene before her—like a puzzle piece that didn't fit right, or a picture containing one small item that didn't quite belong—scratched at Lottie's mind, urging her to figure it out, to put the right pieces together.

Mrs. Hale was a housekeeper, but she also turned the complex knobs and controls on the machine like an expert engineer. Someone who understood it deeply and knew how it worked.

Lottie looked to the empty place where Hale's magic was supposed to be.

"Who did you lose?" Lottie asked, fighting to keep her voice steady. "On the day I met my uncle, you said you lost someone, too. Who was it?"

Mrs. Hale didn't answer. She stared at Lottie, nostrils flared, her face a stone-cold blank slate.

And the truth began to push its way through. It started as a fog inside Lottie, a shapeless, shifting thing. Then it coiled and wound together, taking the tightening, twirling form of a tornado.

Hale knew how the machinery worked, not because

she had been taught, but because she had *built* it. And Hale didn't have magic, but not because it went out when she turned Living Gray. Hale didn't have magic because it was *never* there to start with.

"It's Dalia, isn't it?" Lottie asked softly. "That's who you've lost."

A tear, shining like a shard of glass, slipped down the gray lady's cheek.

"Yes." The polished voice of Mrs. Hale disappeared, and a grating, low, guttural sound erupted from her throat. Something more animal than human.

Which made sense, because Mrs. Hale wasn't a person at all—

She was Warwick's splinter.

A manifestation of it, something that came into being when his magic twisted, breaking off from the source. The Stone Man had turned to stone, because he wished to never feel again. And her uncle received a life sentence in the In Between, because he wished to be reunited with his dead wife.

Splintered magic lies.

Hale had been lying to them all, the entire time. Like with the Stone Man and his children, she had been taking advantage of their sadness, pulling people into a devastating situation like a spider collecting prey inside its web. Gathering as many souls as she could possibly ruin before it was over.

Hale's eyes rolled back inside her head.

Lottie's skin crawled and she pressed her back against the wall, feeling for but failing to find the opening to the staircase.

When her eyes returned, smoldering flames danced in the place Hale's pupils used to be. Her fingers withered and crumpled into charred bits of bone, like the black on the tree in the garden before the ice covered it over. Her gray hair burst free from its tight coil and fell in limp, stringy clumps around her head. The skin pulled back from her face, then dissolved into dust, leaving only a gray skull with patches of skin hanging from her chin and forehead and cheeks.

Hale had been right—splintered magic, especially when angry, was the ugliest thing in the world.

"Congratulations," Hale—or the splintered magic that went by Hale—growled. "You clever, troublesome girl."

Mrs. Hale's charred, smoking fingers pulled out the watch from her pocket. "I would have been so content to let Warwick wander the In Between for as many years as his body would hold him. It's been so. Much. *Fun.* Watching him wasting away to nothing, searching a sea of ghosts. Having the chance to encourage him—*Oh* yes, Warwick, you'll find her. You'll certainly find her," Hale snarled, revealing a set of pointy, gray, jagged teeth. "I do so love the clever deals you humans try to make, like that poor stone man and countless others." She opened the watch and peered at the time. "It started so small at first for him, just a little bit heavier, a little stiffer each day. He almost didn't notice anything at all, it happened so slowly. And then one day, he could barely lift himself out of bed and he *knew*. He ran to the park with his children, crying and screaming for help, but it was too late. Just like you. Just like now. *Whoops, I shouldn't have gone chasing after ghosts, tethering myself to my uncle's splinter.* And now you won't survive the night."

"What?!" Everything inside Lottie wanted to bolt down the stairs and warn the others. But she summoned her strength. She needed to know what Hale was planning so they could try to find a way to stop it.

"You've gone and ruined things, Lottie. You couldn't just let sorrow be sorrow, let gray be gray." She clicked the watch shut. "And now your time is up, we've arrived at the end of the game."

"What game?!" Lottie screamed. "My life isn't a game. Clement, my uncle, Agnes. Our lives aren't *games*."

The vat churned and the level rose, enough for both of them to see it.

Hale leaned over the sorrow. She rolled back her fiery eyes and inhaled. Then she stuck out a pointy gray tongue and licked her mouth, like she was starving and had just stumbled upon a feast.

Lottie kicked the stone floor. She bit her bottom lip hard to keep herself from crying. She had thought she was helping some great cause when she came here. She thought they were all in it together—pursuing something noble, seeking to find what had been lost.

But now she understood.

If this was a game, it had been rigged against her from the start. She was just a pawn.

And Lottie didn't want her sorrow used against her anymore.

"A game, a bargain, a promise. Call it what you will, but you all agreed to come here to be reunited with the ones you've lost. And splintered magic always holds up its end. Want to no longer feel? Turn into stone. Filled with regret? Forget everything and everyone you hurt along the way and all the memories that went with them. Desperate to find someone to love as beautiful as you are? Fall in love with your own reflection." Hale's voice deepened even further, sounding more like a team of voices than the voice of one. "We've been around for centuries, dear, and we're in the business of making wishes come true."

Hale flicked her wrist, and the lever controlling the amount of sorrow going into the machine cranked downward with a sharp creak. Sorrow drained from the vat into the piping, and the gears began to turn. They clicked and clanked into each other as a steady flow of steam escaped, screaming like a boiling teapot from a hatch out the top.

"This isn't what any of us meant!" Lottie shouted as Forsaken began to rumble. "You twist words and intentions! You take magic and turn it into something it was never meant to be!"

"Perhaps I do," Hale said, her voice seething like a legion of devils. "But what did you honestly think would happen?"

Lottie paused and watched Hale's writhing, smoking form, and she saw it so plainly, so clearly, for the very first time. Splintered magic was magic that had broken off from the source of beauty and goodness and life. And because of it, splintered magic couldn't reflect any of those things anymore. In fact, it became the opposite of what it was intended to be. And, therefore, splintered magic could only be ugly, and bad, and destructive.

Lottie's own magic shook, but it was still there, and it was still warm. It still shone the color of gold. *Her* magic was pure. It was good, and was meant to add brightness to a world that was sometimes very hard but could hold so much beauty, too.

Hale looked upon Lottie with mock pity. "I'm sorry to say it's taken you far too long to sort it all out. It was too late for you the moment you decided to take *my* hand. You see, Lottie, the fact of the matter is that the only way to reunite you with the ones you've lost is if you cross through the great Veil to Ever After. All souls end up there eventually, and so eventually you'll be reunited. I'd hoped to let you all wander here for years and years, suck the sorrow out of you slowly over time." She shrugged, a reluctant letting go. "But seeing as you've gone and taken away my fuel, we'll need to get to Ever After quickly, before we run out. There, you'll find your parents, and Dalia, and even Timmy at some point."

"I don't want to chase ghosts anymore." Lottie's words came out weaker than she'd hoped. Too much like pleading. She tried again, forcing a bravery she didn't truly feel. "But I don't understand how going to the mountains is much different from what we've been doing. Except that we'd be waiting there for the ghosts to come to us, instead of looking for them."

"Oh my." Mrs. Hale's voice snapped back to its former ladylike tone, though the skin still hung off her face and her eyes still burned. "You don't see how serious this is, do you."

The tornado in Lottie's stomach spun its mighty wind, sending snaking dread and bloodcurdling terror blasting through her soul. She thought of all the things she and Clement had hoped for while they healed in the garden, the biggest of which was that splintered magic might have a hope of healing, too. And now here she was, staring splintered magic right in the face. It reeked of havoc and hatred and a warped sense of right and wrong.

Hale dusted her hands against her skirt, sweat slicking along her chin and dotting across the lingering skin on her forehead.

Lottie's muscles grew rigid. Her blood froze like ice in her veins. Her heart stopped beating as Mrs. Hale made very clear what this trip would cost her.

"To get into Ever After," Hale hissed, "you can't still be alive."

THE VEIL

Forsaken retched like it never had before, something savage and ruthless, far worse than the initial groanings that had startled Lottie so much during her first days here.

No. This was different.

This was a *the world is ripping apart at the seams, the walls will crumble around you, the earth will break open and swallow you whole* kind of quaking.

Terrified, Lottie braced herself against the wall to keep from falling. The sound of her heartbeat thrashed in her ears and her nails scratched against the stone as she tried to find something, anything to hold on to.

Her father's words from so many years ago echoed in her mind.

Those who splinter never survive.

Hale flicked her wrist sharply, and the lever cranked even further, shooting all the remaining sorrow through the piping and setting the gears to spin like tops.

Lottie *wilted*. Mrs. Hale had just set her deadly plans into horrifying motion. And every friend she had in this whole entire world was down in the garden, completely unaware.

She had to warn them.

Lottie bolted down the stairs.

"Not so fassst." As Lottie stumbled down the final steps, the hissing team of voices that came from the throat of the thing she had known as Hale slithered past.

In the blink of an eye, the door to the hall slammed shut in front of Lottie's face.

Then the lock turned with a firm *thunk*.

Lottie jangled at the doorknob, trying to force it to turn until she heard the magical engine kick on from somewhere deep inside the belly of Forsaken. She turned a desperate gaze toward the tower, then darted back up the steps and past the room with the gears.

Hale, her back to the door as she worked on the machinery, cackled as Lottie climbed past.

Lottie reached the top of the tower as the shuddering grew to a jolting that shifted even the stones beneath her feet.

Clear tears fell down her cheeks, and her heart broke

into a thousand tiny pieces. She didn't have enough time—enough time to warn them, let alone save them. So she knelt in front of the window, bracing herself as the In Between fell into a blur and they raced off to the mountains at breakneck speed.

By the time her friends realized what was happening, it would be too late.

The mountains loomed closer by the second. They filled more and more of the window frame, growing wide and tall and imposing. It was as if she were on a train track, watching a great steam engine bear down, mere moments from running her over.

The leagues of ghosts scattered in a panic, tumbling over each other as they ran to either side of Forsaken's surge.

Just like on the day she left the Land of the Living and crossed into the In Between, a thin curtain appeared in the air, stretching downward from the sky. It shifted, as if caught up in a light wind. Slightly white but mostly transparent, this Veil billowed and waved, a too-cheerful greeting to their arrival. It stood, slow and soft in a world hazy with movement.

Lottie squeezed her eyes shut and held on tight. They were about to plow it through like a bull into a cape.

Until they didn't.

Because instead of going through it, Forsaken slammed into the Veil.

A horrendous *BOOM*, like a firework bursting right next to Lottie's head, like the final heartbeat of the whole entire world, consumed Forsaken.

Lottie flew backward from the force of the impact. Her back slapped onto the floor just a few feet from the window.

She covered her head as the glass shattered, then tinkled down like tiny diamonds.

The scuttle of maggots, and beetles, and spiders thrown from their shadowy crevices clicked and clopped as they scrambled to re-hide.

Then, all that had roared and groaned and shook fell utterly silent.

Lottie opened her eyes and uncovered her head. A cloud of debris and dust floated a moment and then settled around her, painting her with a filmy layer of gray and brown. She listened for any sign of the gray lady in the room with the gears below.

Nothing.

She had to hope the crash had at least thrown off Mrs. Hale enough to buy a bit of extra time.

Lottie crunched against something as she turned. Curled-in bits of once-glowing scroll, now burnt down to only singed flecks of dull paper, lay scattered all over the floor.

The Ledger of Souls. Or, what was left of it.

Of course. Mrs. Hale had acquired it for her uncle. She had used it as a prop to get them all exactly where she wanted. It had played its part, and now it was gone.

Lottie dusted herself off as best she could and turned back to the now-broken window.

Her mouth fell open and her hand flew to clutch the locket at her chest.

Any hesitation, any doubt she had ever felt about Ever After disappeared in an instant. There would be no more worry about whether Ever After was good or bad, because it was, without question, the most beautiful thing Lottie would ever see.

She watched as every ghost close to the mountains sprinted toward the Veil, their arms outstretched to the sky, pure elation on their faces as they ran through it. None of them hesitated here at the border. Not when they could see inside. Each of them ran like a child into a parent's loving, open arms.

And Lottie could see why.

Abundant trees stood tall and crystal-blue waterfalls flowed. Soft music playing, piano and strings and choruses of voices, reached out through the curtain. Along with a host of things Lottie didn't even have words for, at least not in the language people spoke. But they were things she would carry in her heart for the rest of her days.

And then Lottie saw something that took her breath clear away—

As the souls crossed through the curtain, they lifted into the air and a bright red cardinal burst forth from their hearts. The birds turned and soared, bright wings spread wide, back through the Veil and then onward, in the direction Lottie had come from so many months ago. Straight toward Vivelle.

Back before she turned gray, Lottie had once thought it was a nice story, about the cardinals and what they meant. But first with her book, and now again with the cardinals, she had discovered that something she thought was just a story was, in fact, very real. The cardinals *were* messengers from Ever After, to let their loved ones know they had made it safely home.

Lottie's magic flared as hope swelled inside her.

And she knew for certain: If everyone is born with a measure of magic, and if magic, when used as it's meant to be used, adds beauty and good to the world, and if the Great Magician is the one to bestow it . . . then Ever After, the home of the Great Magician, well . . . of course it would be the most beautiful and good thing there ever was.

But that didn't change the fact that they weren't meant to be here yet. They were still alive. They belonged in the Land of the Living.

Lottie smiled to herself. Maybe that was why they crashed *into* the Veil instead of through it. Maybe the Great Magician wouldn't let them in. Because it wasn't their time.

Lottie's tight, sore muscles finally let go of the tension they'd been holding since the moment she realized Timmy was Agnes's brother. She imagined her friends, just out of sight, tucked away in the garden, doing the same.

But she couldn't relax for long.

Just then, on the In Between side of the Veil, a group of dark clouds pulled together, then set themselves to swirling directly in front of the window and above Lottie's head.

A crack of thunder sounded and Forsaken trembled as a flash of lightning struck the tower.

A harsh whispering wound up the spiral staircase, making Lottie's hair stand on end.

No. This wasn't over yet. She was safe for the moment, but Hale hadn't sent them through the Veil, which meant something far more serious: Hale wasn't done.

Forsaken's engine sputtered, then revved back to life. This time the shaking loosened several stones from their places on the walls. In front of the window, a smattering of shingles fell like birds with broken wings, tumbling to the ground outside the tower.

The outermost wall, where Lottie had sat for so many weeks searching for her parents, buckled against the Veil, the brick bending inward like a snapped bone.

Lottie looked on with horror as Forsaken pushed *into* the Veil.

She couldn't take this any longer. She ran back down to the room with the gears. The groaning and shaking continued, getting worse by the second, breaking the earth beneath them and sending the shriek of stone grinding against metal into the air.

Lottie's nostrils flared and anger surged inside her at the sight of Hale, singed and horrid, still tinkering with a set of knobs and gauges, her movements edged with tension. Lottie had understood so little at the time, but now, seeing this, she couldn't imagine how she'd ever let herself be deceived into thinking splintered magic could be in any way good.

Smoke rolled out from the bottom of Hale's skirt

and her neck crackled as it snapped toward the door. Her eyes, all fire and speckled over with thin gray veins, like the broken shell of a spoiled egg, set their sights on Lottie. A growl escaped from deep in Hale's throat, the kind of sound that lived in nightmares, the ones weighted with blackness and reeking of rot and blood's metallic tang.

Hale turned away from Lottie and shook herself back into focus on the work before her. She jumped to grab hold of the long lever and then pulled on it with all the weight in her scorched body, her charred feet dangling inches from the floor.

The metal screeched, then bent, slowly at first, then at a sharper and sharper angle, before breaking off entirely, shooting a hollow clank through the room as it landed.

Lottie clenched her fists. They might not be able to enter Ever After while still alive, but she hated that this had been Hale's endgame the whole entire time. That she had set the price of splintered magic, for all of them, to be the loss of their very lives. Soon, Forsaken would crumble as it pushed against the barrier to the mountains. First, the outer wall would fall, then the gardens, and then the entire house. Forsaken would survive the effort about as well as a sandcastle survives the tide. Hale would bury them all in the rubble, or, if they managed to somehow survive the estate's collapse, the protective enchantment would dissolve around the ruins, and they'd suffocate immediately in the hostile In Between air.

Splintered magic was going to win, unless they could find a way to stop it.

But Lottie was alone, like the fragile Bunch in the garden. Like the tearstained pillows, the wilted flowers, the cold wind whipping across her cheeks through the window in Vivelle. This was alone like all of those times, and worse, and more. This was the kind of alone she wouldn't survive. She needed to get to her friends.

She needed to break down the door.

Lottie made a dash for the stairs as the tower trembled around her. Her side hit the wall and her legs tripped over themselves as she stumbled down. But it didn't matter. She had to get free.

She used the momentum from her descent to slam her entire body into the thick, heavy wood of the door's bottom half. Once, twice, a third time, more. Until her shoulder screamed.

Then, in a moment, and only for a moment, all grew eerily still.

"Don't bother," a voice slithered. "It's enchanted to keep you in." Lottie turned to stare in horror as the nightmare that was Hale floated down the staircase, carrying a flickering, ghostly candelabra in her outstretched hand. She glided past Lottie and straight through the door, leaving a wake of shock-cold air behind her.

Splintered magic personified stopped and glared in at her through the barred window while Lottie watched, powerless, from behind the narrow iron grates.

THE GREAT TANGLE

"Your uncle's nearly arrived, and just in time." Hale leaned in close and breathed hot, sour breath in Lottie's face. "Unlike you, *he* won't have the pleasure of feeling the floor drop out from under his feet. He'll remain right outside Forsaken's gates, gray hands clutched round the cold, metal bars, watching everything he's built crumble."

Hale arranged her features into the closest thing to a smile that her grotesque face could conjure. "I've been with him this whole time, in one way or another. Smoldering in his chest. Ensuring a steady source of fuel while he's away. And I'm going to be there as he watches it end. The moment he realizes he never should have splintered. That he should have released the grip on his magic long ago, and accepted the suffering he'd been offered. Which will be the exact same moment he realizes it's just. Too. Late."

She took a final satisfied peek at her clock. Then she floated down the hall like a specter, her long gray skirt swishing through the air.

Leaving Lottie locked in the tower.

As soon as Hale disappeared around the corner, Lottie screamed. She screamed for all of the times she was frightened but thought no one would hear her or care. For the way she'd been manipulated and used. And for the fact that she'd just learned that she could heal, and was still working so hard to fight for her magic and her color. She had learned that hope was possible and she was willing to take the risk of opening her heart again, to keep her magic glowing strong. But she wanted more *time*. She needed more time. She deserved to have all the time in the world.

Lottie sunk to the floor, sliding her back against the wood, then let her head fall into her hands. She was only a girl with tired, gray-tipped arms and limp, gray-tipped hair and a weak, gray-tipped heart. She had wanted to believe that splintered magic could heal, that they might be able to undo what had been done once her uncle knew that healing was an option. Once he saw how hope had taken root in his son.

She had even wondered if someday they might go back to Vivelle, and if she might find a way to use her magic to bring good and beauty to the living world.

But her uncle wasn't here and Hale was a thief. She had stolen Lottie's chance. Snatched it. Broken it.

Left it splintered.

If a fairy, or a magical being of any kind, had appeared to Lottie at that exact moment and granted her one single wish, she would wish she had never come to Forsaken. Hale had asked her, and had even told her that she had a choice before she made her decision. Lottie *knew* she was signing on to splintered magic, but now she realized she wasn't any better than the children who had followed their father into the park and held on to his hand as they all turned to stone.

Father.

It had only been months, but her last date with her own dad, when they went out for cider the night the fall fires burned . . . it felt like a thousand years ago now.

She hadn't ever thought she was much like him, at least not in certain, important ways. He led with his brain, she led with her heart. She had often wished she had a bit more *him* inside her, even when things weren't so very hard.

Lottie lifted her head.

She clicked open her locket and stared at the two people she missed more than anything in the whole entire world. She ran her thumb along the glass covering her father's face. The thumb still stained with smears of color from her painting earlier that very same day under the burnt, thawed tree, made with her gray, healing heart. She stared at his crinkle-at-the-edges-when-he-smiled eyes.

They had always been similar in that way, at least. Her eyes crinkled, too, whenever she smiled.

If her father were here, he'd know how to fix this.

Lottie's thoughts drifted over everything she'd been through. And then she realized—she had actually solved a lot of problems herself since coming to Forsaken. It had taken both her brain and her heart to find the key to the garden, and to help it thaw. Even though she'd realized it too late, it had also taken both head and heart to call out Mrs. Hale for who, or what, she really was.

Maybe she was more like her father than she'd once thought.

And her father never stopped trying, even when a problem made him feel like his head was going to explode. Even when it took him a lot of wrong turns and a very long time.

Lottie's magic shimmered.

Maybe if she kept trying, she could figure this out, too.

She couldn't be with her parents again in the Land of the Living, but that didn't mean they were fully gone. She carried pieces of them inside of her. And if she could fix things now, then maybe her magic could still have a chance to bring good and beauty to the world—like her mother had done with the garden and flowers—and like her parents always believed she would.

Nellie had told Lottie she wasn't anything special. And she'd been right in some ways, but not completely. Lottie wasn't any more or less special than anyone else, both when she had her color and when she faded. But she *was* special. She was special because everyone was exceptional and unique, and the world would miss out on something very important without her in it.

Lottie snapped the locket shut and gave it a hug with her hand before letting go. She stomped up to the top of the tower and stared out the broken window, at the wall, buckling under the pressure from the Veil. Forsaken creaked like a worn ship on the verge of capsizing.

She could see the gate she had entered through on her first night here. There her uncle stood, just as Hale said he would. His stone-gray face had fallen ashen. One hand clutched the locked gates and the other one clutched his heart. His mouth was open, but Lottie couldn't hear his sorrowful cries over the rest of the clamor. His splintered magic both smoldered in his chest and floated above and off to the side of him as Hale. The bottom of her skirt had ripped ragged and her hair now swirled and twisted in the wind like a swarm of oily gray snakes.

Lottie forced her gaze away from the part of this that she couldn't control and focused on the things she could. The window had broken in the initial collision, which meant she didn't have to waste precious time finding a way to break it herself.

Then she licked her lips and sent out an airy whistle, mimicking Timmy's whistle as best she could. And she hoped. And because she hoped, her magic grew.

Within moments, a blur of red blew in through the broken window.

"There you are, Mr. Cardinal!" Lottie's heart surged as her friend circled the room, chirruping and trilling wildly, like he knew they didn't have any time to waste. "I need you to tell them that I'm locked in the tower. Tell them I need my satchel. As *fast* as you can. I'll be waiting at the door. Go!"

The cardinal zoomed away, straight as an arrow, like a red bolt of lightning from the tower down toward the garden walls. In the same instant, the outside wall crumbled completely, sending a pile of bricks and rubble across the outermost paths. Forsaken reared back, then shoved into the Veil again, relentless on its road toward self-destruction.

Lottie ran down to the door just in time to see an entire section of estate crumble at the end of the hall. What once had been a twisting series of corridors and rooms fell away, leaving a set of stairs that opened up to a dark sky and spinning debris—chair legs, a fireplace poker, several dozen playing cards, the portrait of the crying lady.

Lottie searched the deepest part of the well inside her—scraping it, gathering anything that was left. Trembling, she closed her eyes and imagined setting the remainders of her courage right next to her magic. She hoped it would help her see this through.

"Lottie!" A pair of voices sounded from the still-standing set of stairs near the tower.

Agnes. And Clement.

"The cardinal landed on your satchel and wouldn't stop tugging it, like he was trying to lift it into the air!" Agnes yelled over the noise as they arrived at the door. "Then he circled the tower, so we'd know where to find you!"

Lottie pumped a fist through the air in triumph. She knew he could do it. She knew the cardinal would help.

Clement opened the satchel and he and Agnes began sliding paints and brushes through the grates as quickly as they could. Last, they passed her the empty satchel, and Lottie gathered all the supplies inside it on her side of the door.

Her stomach clenched as another great quaking ravaged Forsaken. She, Clement, and Agnes all braced themselves to keep from falling. The sound of paintings shaking off walls and statues tipping and crashing onto the floor ricocheted through the once-grand estate. Bits of rock crumbled down from the ceiling. Lightning flashed again and thunder clapped so loud it felt like it was coming from inside her.

This might be it.

She couldn't fail.

"Whatever you're doing, good luck," Clement said. Agnes gave a quick, nervous nod.

Lottie reached her fingers through the grate and gave their hands a gentle squeeze before turning away. She hoped they would make it out safely. Then she bounded up the stairs, two, three at a time, carrying her satchel across her shoulder.

Another roar sounded, followed by a crash as more of Forsaken fell.

She didn't have much time.

Lottie ran into the room with the gears, and the sky blackened like someone had snuffed out a candle.

It took her eyes a moment to adjust, but when she did, she saw that the room, which should have fallen under the same sudden darkness as the world outside, wasn't, in fact, lightless.

Lottie could still *see*. She turned one way, then another, seeking out a candle, or something else that might be lending light to the room. But there was nothing. She looked all around, and up and down—and then she saw it.

Her *magic*, the color of melted gold, glowed from inside her and radiated out. It pulsed like a second heartbeat, full and warm and strong. She tiptoed around broken glass and torn pages and snippets of spells on parchment, finally setting down her satchel next to the mess of turning gears.

She opened it up and pulled out her paints, then stared down at the vat of sorrow that had partly refilled itself during all the fear and chaos. She closed her eyes and inhaled.

Sorrow itself wasn't a bad thing when in its right place. It meant she had loved—and *still* loved—her parents with her whole, entire heart. It meant that her friends and family here loved deeply, too. But sorrow wasn't meant to be leeched out of people and collected together and used for something destructive.

Her uncle had told her using it here, like *this*, gave her sorrow purpose. But that was just another one of splintered magic's lies. Her sorrow had meaning because it *meant* she was human. That she had loved and that she had lost. She didn't need for it to have any more meaning than that, even though it had. Her sorrow had brought her to Clement, and connected her to Agnes, and even to Timmy. Her sorrow was a part of her now, though it wouldn't always be the biggest part. It would fit into different-sized places over time, leaving space for things like hope, and laughter, and magic to settle back in and have room to breathe. Her sorrow had helped her to learn how much she was willing to fight to keep her magic, beautiful and good like it was meant to be, no matter how many times in her life she had to work to heal.

And it taught her how much it meant to fight for her life right now.

Her uncle had set this terrible, grim, splintered magic into motion.

But Lottie had magic, too. And she was going to stop it.

Lottie had learned a lot about color in her twelve years of living. She knew that blue and yellow made green, and red and yellow made orange, and red and blue made purple. She knew that white was the reflection of the entire spectrum of colors and black was the absence of light.

And right here, in this moment, she would add light to the sorrow, and she would do it by painting *hope.*

She would inject hope. Imbue hope. Instill it. She would take all of the magic inside her and knot it together with hope more than she ever had before.

Lottie picked up a jar of paint and poured it into the vat, careful not to spill a single drop.

Orange for the sherbet she and Clement would share at Felicity's Enchanted Treats next summer.

She picked up another.

Pink for the sunsets she would watch at the edge of Vivelle's endless sea.

Scarlet for the seats at the dance hall where they'd all watch Clement perform.

White for Vivelle's first dust of snow.

Green for the garden she and Clement would nurture together, in honor of those they had lost.

Lottie added a rainbow to the sorrow, each pigment a hope she had for the future, or for the future of one of her friends. She watched as the vat's slow churning absorbed the colors, stirred them, mixed them in. She hoped that the sorrow would be unable to withstand the color infusion.

And then she held her breath.

A sputtering sounded from the tangle of cogs and smoke erupted from an angry valve. The contraption coughed, and Lottie stumbled back.

The sound of a great engine shutting down—of mechanisms and gears and steam halting to a stop—shook the estate one final time.

Then all grew quiet and still.

Lottie looked down at the empty jars of paint littering the floor beside her, and she finally, finally breathed.

"Stand back!"

Lottie turned toward the sound of an axe splintering wood at the bottom of the stairs. Soon Clement, Agnes, Lydia, and George rushed into the room and took in the messy scene.

A vat full of strangely colored liquid, a large set of clogged and broken gears, and, in the middle of it all, a paint-stained girl with a light in her eyes and a smile on her face.

A FINAL GOODBYE

Forsaken's tower creaked and swayed like it hung from a single, tired hinge. Its remaining stone walls slouched, half-buckled in, half-splayed open, dripping decomposed muck down their sides. It reminded Lottie of the Beast of Burden she had ridden on the day she arrived here. It had looked so polished and regal at first, but underneath all that leather and velvet was a mess of maggots and decay. There was no denying anymore that splintered magic poisoned everything it touched. Forsaken had been rotting from the inside out for years. And now only its skin remained, emptied of the muscles and bones required to hold it together.

After a brief reunion, Lottie had sent her friends back to the garden, and now she ran, fast as she could, alone to the gate. There Warwick lingered, shocked and shaking, his gray hand clutching iron, still locked outside.

"Lottie!" he called out, his voice hoarse from lack of

use. His worn cape sagged around his sharp shoulders, and his clothes dangled off his skeletal frame.

"I'm here!" Lottie slowed to a stop on the other side and wrapped her warming, half-gray hand around her uncle's icy cold one. She remembered what the all-consuming gray had felt like inside herself, but she had to force herself to not rip her hand back the moment she touched his brittle, frigid skin.

Warwick inhaled a ragged breath. "My splinter—" he stuttered. "It's gone."

Lottie took in his shaking body and hollow chest, then let go of his hand and worked to unlock the gate. She could still breathe fine, so the enchantment over Forsaken must have been strong enough to hold through all that had happened. But Warwick was right. The smoldering magic that had allowed him to survive the harsh In Between air had extinguished completely. It now rested tired and flat and lifeless as used-up coals inside his chest.

She released the lock and lifted the latch, and the wide gates swung open with a creak. Her uncle stumbled inside, gasping roughly before crumpling to the ground. Lottie shut and locked the gate behind him, then ran to Warwick's side.

"I'm fine, Lottie," he said, once his breathing finally settled. "You arrived just in time." He gave the weakest smile Lottie had ever seen, then waved her off as he coughed into his sleeve.

Lottie backed away and gave him a bit of room as he recovered. Then she looked around.

It seemed that her uncle's smoldering magic wasn't the only thing that had disappeared.

Her sights caught on a glint of something silver, just to the side of the gate. She ran over to it to get a closer look.

On the dirt lay Mrs. Hale's precious silver pocket watch.

It was all that remained of the gray lady, the manifestation of her uncle's splinter. The one who had tormented this place and the people inside it, for such a long time. Lottie picked up the watch by its heavy chain, then clicked it open. There she found, where the watch face should have been, a small hourglass instead. A large crack leading to a chunk of missing glass marred its curved, clear surface. All the sand from inside it had disappeared and blown away.

Her father had told her that splintered magic was a clock, counting down the moments until a person's destruction. Whatever clock had been running against Warwick and the rest of them had mercifully paused, at least for now.

It was a good sign, but Lottie couldn't be sure yet that the threat against them was entirely snuffed out. At least not until she found a flicker of something still remaining, not splintered, in her uncle's chest.

She wasn't ready for what might happen if the smolder still lingered in there somewhere, or worse, if his magic had completely gone out. But she would look again when he was in the garden, *after* he saw Clement. Not a moment sooner than that.

A SHORT WHILE LATER, LOTTIE AND HER UNCLE STEPPED foot through the magical arched entrance.

As Lottie expected, the enchanted garden had suffered its share of damage. The Tickles' hive lay broken open on the ground like a smashed yellow melon. Thin branches had snapped off from nearby trees and now lay scattered along the garden floor. The flowers stood hunched or flattened like they had been trampled by a giant.

A stunned Henry Warwick took the garden in while Lottie mourned the wreckage. She bent to the earth and lifted up a shattered petal from one of the Bunches. She held it in the palm of her hand, then turned to her uncle.

"Losing this garden was part of the price of the splinter," he said, his voice low and haunting. "Dalia loved it so much; it was a part of her. I couldn't bear to lose this piece of her, too."

"Is that why you cast it in ice?" Lottie asked him. "To somehow preserve it?"

Warwick let out a deep sigh. "I wish I could take the credit, but I didn't play any part in protecting the garden. The garden found a way to protect itself from *me*. This place was built of too good a stuff, too pure a magic. It couldn't coexist with me . . . not once my magic splintered. The last time I saw it, on the day that she died, plumes of black smoke swept up into the sky from the tree at the center. I was certain it would crumble to ash behind me. I couldn't bear to watch, so I left it to burn."

Lottie gently set the shattered petal back on the soil, dusted off her palms, then stood. "When I found it, it was still burned and nearly dead, but it had frozen over before it was completely destroyed. It must have been enchanted with some very powerful magic to keep itself safe if something bad happened, at least until the right people came along to bring it back to life."

"You mean, you did this?" her uncle asked. "*You* brought the garden back to life?"

"Not by myself. All of this," Lottie gestured toward the lingering greens and warm colors, "I did with your son."

Warwick's deep-set eyes widened, revealing an ocean of regret.

They had set all their hopes on the moment her uncle returned and found the garden filled with mysterious sunshine, and vibrant greens, and popping pinks, and striking blues. The warm orange of the butterflies and the yellow flicker of the Tickles as they alighted on a flower. The dawn breaking through Forsaken's long, dark night.

But this, the garden, beaten and bruised after surviving a second disaster, would have to do.

As they stood there together, ever so softly, the music of the garden kicked up a tranquil, hopeful song. The pulse of life, the flap of wings, the Tickles' buzz, rose above all that had broken. And over the top, a boy's singing, a gentle tenor, in perfect time and harmony with the garden around it, lilted from just around the bend.

"Go on," Lottie said. "Clement is waiting for you to find him."

Warwick set his sights forward, then sprinted ahead.

Lottie followed close behind as the path broke open. Clement spun in his dancing shoes, moving to and singing along with the life all around him. The song set into motion by his mother, before he was even born.

Her uncle stepped on a branch, cracking it under his

feet. Clement froze in place, his back to them both, and the whole garden fell quiet.

"I've found you." Warwick reached out his arms.

Clement turned and stared at his father, at the shell of him, at least. Then he leapt forward, the kind of giant leap that swallows half a dozen normal-sized steps inside it. Warwick's thin arms wrapped around Clement. He touched his son's face as gentle tears filled both their eyes, then fell.

"I wasn't lost, you know." Clement pulled back and set his own hands on his father's stone-colored cheeks. "I've been waiting. I've been here the whole entire time."

Warwick collapsed to his knees and buried his face in his son's shoulder. The un-graying boy and his gray father sat together beneath the tree to Lottie's left, without words, for a long while.

To her right, Agnes and her parents and Timmy gathered in the middle of their own strange reunion.

Lottie hesitated, standing still and alone between the two families, connected to both but not fully a part of either. Uncertainty sent uneasy waves through her stomach. She didn't quite know where her place was in this picture.

Clement turned to Lottie and waved her over. She walked slowly, then sat beside them under the tree.

She swallowed, then forced herself to meet her cousin's eye—to bear head-on the happiness, the joy, and the relief written all over his face. Seeing parents with their children would likely always be hard, at least in some ways. But the sinking feeling at the fresh reminder of her loss felt less like a boulder collapsing off a cliff than it had before. Now it felt more like the kind of sinking you get when riding over the top of a hill too fast. Still there, still noticeable, but a little more tolerable, too. It wouldn't bury her under its weight today.

"Look at us," her uncle said. "My son, dancing like his mother. My niece . . . the garden." He paused and looked all around him. "It's survived much worse than the events of today." He tucked a strand of moppy hair behind his ear. "But how did you do it, Lottie? You were just as faded as any of us when you arrived. How in the world did you bring such a change?"

"It wasn't just me—"

"But it *was*, Lottie," interrupted Clement. "If you hadn't come, I'd never have left my room. We'd have wasted away out here for years and years, and then when Hale had used us all up, she would have crashed us into the Veil, over and over, until nothing was left. Forsaken would have been destroyed. *We* would have been gone. You need to tell him how *you* saved us."

How she had saved them.

Lottie closed her eyes and let those words sink in deep. A long time ago in a place far away from here, her parents had said that splintered magic was so very powerfully bad only because the original purpose for magic was so very powerfully good. And her little golden magic, the gift that was uniquely and specially hers, had overcome splintered magic at its absolute worst.

So Lottie told him their story. And as she finished up, the great, enchanted tree shook its branches, rich and full with thick, emerald-green leaves.

Warwick stood and walked over to it, running a hand along its trunk.

"The tree helped us," Lottie said. "It helped us know where to start."

The tree shook again, sending a marvelous, rich scent through the air.

"It's a wonder," Warwick said. "Though I'm not surprised. Your mothers walked through this garden with round bellies, imagining the day their children would play and grow together inside its walls. They prepared a way for you, built something so filled with love that not even a splinter could destroy it, long before they ever knew you'd need it this much."

Lottie's heart soared. She had known her mother's

love for her this entire time, but she would never get tired of the stories of the garden and the thoughtful ways she'd prepared a path forward for Lottie before she'd even been born.

"They were wise to keep you away from me once I splintered," Warwick said. He rubbed his weary eyes and leaned against the tree, his fatigue finally catching up to him after years without any sleep. "Your mother gave up this side of the family, and the garden, in order to keep you safe from all that splintered magic brings. I'm sorry you found your way here, but also, I agree with Clement. I can't help but think if you hadn't, we'd all still be lost."

The cardinal hopped down from where it had been hiding. It set itself on a nearby branch, then took off and circled Warwick's head, filling the air with its trilling.

"Mr. Cardinal!" Clement's face lit up as he, too, stood.

"Have you see them, Clement?" Lottie jumped up to join him. "When the souls cross over, have you seen the cardinals burst out of their hearts?!"

"Yes, we all saw it!" Clement grinned as the bird circled his head next.

"Looks like he's found who he's meant to get a message to." Timmy walked over to the tree with his family close behind him. He turned to Warwick. "I think you've got yourself a sign."

Warwick looked up at the bird, his face a swirl of questions.

"A sign . . . from Dalia." He spoke at nearly a whisper. "So it's true, then, what they say about cardinals."

"Yes," said Clement. "He's here to tell us that Mother is safe, and well. She's home."

The cardinal landed on Clement's held-out finger. He wiped away a fat, heavy tear, then gave a gentle pat to the bird's head.

"I never wanted you to lose her." Warwick's voice broke. "A child needs his mother."

"I know. I miss her all the time. But I hope you'll stay now, Father. Because I need *you*, too. And you'll have to find a way to be enough."

"For both of us," Lottie added, letting the ache of loss rise, then crest, then ebb inside her heart.

Timmy turned toward where souls lifted into the air and cardinals burst forth from their chests as they crossed over. Lottie had gotten very used to seeing him stare off at the mountains as their weeks in the garden went on. The ghost boy had changed, since even the start of that very day. He no longer looked like merely a ghost. His form now waved, and shimmered, and a gentle light reflected off his transparent cheeks.

Lottie reached out her hand and passed it through his, giving it a squeeze and hoping that, somehow, he could feel it.

"You're leaving us now, aren't you," she said.

"I am." Timmy watched the mountains. "You were right, Lottie. I was feeling pulled there this whole entire time." He turned back to the people gathered around him, then wiggled his toes and gave a quick sniff. "I wasn't ready to trust it then, but I am now. I know that it's good."

George and Lydia nodded, and did their best to look strong.

Agnes let her own tears fall, which led a smattering of tiny flowers to sprout up beneath her feet. She shook her head in amazement, then looked back at her brother. "We'll see you off," she said.

A DISCARDED PILE OF HEMLOCK LAY ON THE GROUND OUT-side the wall and, for the first time in years, Timmy stepped outside the bounds of the enchanted garden.

The small group made their way to the gates in silence.

Where he once stared wearily toward them, back when the garden was near-dead and frozen, Timmy's eyes now lit up at the sight of Ever After so close.

In a flash, the radiance across his cheeks expanded, and his entire face flooded with light.

Lottie took in all the beautiful things just beyond her reach. Some part of her longed for the mountains, too, in a funny sort of way. But it wasn't the kind of longing that caused the gray, orphan girl from before to stare out over the top of Forsaken's wall and chase after ghosts. It wasn't the kind that wanted to give up, or that had lost its ability to see color and beauty in a living yet broken world.

She had a very important purpose to fulfill during her time on this side of the Veil. Ever After would be there for her someday, long in the future, when her work was done.

"I know things now that I didn't before," Timmy said. "Love is always looking, searching to find a soul who's working through their sorrows, or their struggles, or whatever it is that holds them back. It's not too different from the garden, really. And when it finds you, it helps to mend the holes in your heart. And when a person's holes are mended, then love can fill them up, straight to the top so there's nothing else. When you're ready to be filled, you're ready to cross through the Veil."

Lydia, best as she could, put a hand on her son's cheek, and Agnes brushed her palm across the top of Timmy's hat.

Lottie, Warwick, and Clement stepped back to give the family their last moments together.

Lottie watched Timmy look to Ever After one final time. The radiating light spread through his whole body, reflecting, brighter and brighter, until she couldn't even see him at all without squinting. Then he set off at a run, his arms held up and his eyes fixed forward, straight through the Veil, where he lifted into the air and disappeared.

In moments, a bright red cardinal burst back through the Veil and flew toward Forsaken, landing on a nearby spire. It tipped its head and trilled a song and wiggled its talons from atop its perch.

By the time they turned back to the house, things were already starting to happen.

All around the edge of Forsaken, stones lifted up from the rubble and re-formed themselves into walls. But not the same decayed, cracked, and gray walls as before. The stones transformed as they lifted, turning all sorts of warm shades of brown. The branches of several trees surrounding the house now budded and the sun sent bright rays reflecting off of freshly restored glass.

Lydia and George broke off to check on their small cottage. Warwick took Clement to survey the damage on a walk around the house, which left Lottie and Agnes alone together.

"Can I ask you something?" said Lottie.

"Of course."

"What did it feel like, seeing your brother again, even for a little while?" She twisted her shoe into the dry, powdery soil, too nervous to look Agnes in the eyes.

"It was the strangest thing," Agnes said. "It was my brother; I could see it. I could *feel* it was him. But it was more like meeting the dream of my brother than anything else. He's whole now," she said, her brows set into a determined line. "But he wasn't as a ghost."

Lottie nodded. It made sense, at least as much as something like this could. Her time with Timmy had been an odd blend of feeling like she had a friend, and also feeling like he was never fully there. Timmy's existence in the garden was marked by a palpable tension, a sense of no longer, and also not yet.

Not long ago, Lottie had so badly wanted what Agnes had received. But if Warwick *had* found her parents here, Lottie knew even that, in time, wouldn't have been enough. Living with the ghosts of them would have been a hollow thing. She wouldn't have been able to feel the softness of her mother's hair or the whiskers on her father's chin. Her parents, as she knew and loved them, were both their spirits and their bodies. Like Agnes said, as ghosts, they wouldn't have been whole.

But, in other ways, a dream of her parents, even for a short while, also sounded lovely. Something a bit easier to swallow than having nothing left of them at all.

Though, that wasn't exactly true, either. At least not completely. She couldn't have them the way that she wanted them, there was no way around that. But it didn't mean that she had *nothing*. She could do the things she knew would make them proud, and carry on their legacy in her own life. She could live her life fully, like they would want for her—whether they were here or whether they were gone.

"I think I understand things better now." Lottie pulled her lips to the side. "But in my book, the garden spills over the walls and finds a way to bring healing to the whole entire world. I don't understand how our garden can really do that, and there are so many sad people in the Land of the Living. So many Living Gray."

"Ahh." Agnes tucked a hand into her dress pocket and rocked back on her heels. "That's an important thought, and a good question. Though finding the answer might be complicated and take some time."

"But why? Why can't it just be easy?"

"Well, because I think everyone really has their

own way of healing. Here, in Forsaken, you have a special garden, built of your mother's love and magic and hope. And that's helped you to heal. But my family is different. Our 'garden' is that we talk about Timmy, we find little bits of good in each day, we set about our work with purpose. We let ourselves be sad. For others, maybe their garden is a box filled with special things, or a walk on a sunny day, or a splash in a puddle after a rainstorm. Some might carry their gardens in here." She pointed to the middle of her chest and shrugged. "I think gardens are everywhere, if you know where to look for them. And they do have the power to heal the whole, entire world."

Lottie lost herself in imagining a whole world of healing gardens, in a million colors and a billion different forms—in smiles and laughter, in hugs and held hands, in music and art. She saw it and felt it, deep inside her bones, inside the thing that made her who she was. And she wanted to be a part of it. Whatever that meant, and whatever she had to do to get there.

Lydia reappeared around the corner then, carrying a basket looped through her arm.

"Well, there are plentiful miracles around us, that's for certain," she said, slightly out of breath. "Not the least of which is that our home and this bread and cheese survived all the ruckus."

Lottie's stomach growled and her fingers itched. The rest of the group returned and they all headed back to the enchanted garden together.

There, Lottie helped herself to a wide slice of bread and a thick cut of cheese. She knew exactly what her next painting would be, just as soon as she'd finished her supper.

It would be of a picnic, a family on its way to healing. She would paint a great, vibrant tree with emerald-green leaves, providing shade to a girl and a boy in half gray, half color, and an uncle with a hint of pigment returning to his cheeks. She would paint wide flowering vines advancing over the top of the garden's stone walls behind them, spreading out into the world beyond.

A SHORT WHILE LATER, LOTTIE LAY BACK AND WATCHED HER painting come to life. The vines and flowers grew up the walls and spilled over the other side. The family built of brushstrokes laughed and ate. The garden's music hummed and rustled, and the scent of fresh-baked bread and grass filtered through the painting and into the real-world air. This was a particularly good one.

She stood and hung it from twine off a branch on the tree, then stood back to admire her collection. Over a dozen paintings twirled slowly from their strings, each at different heights. A promising start to a new Lottie's Gallery: The Enchanted Garden Installation.

A deep orange sunset had broken through the In Between's usual flat blanket of clouds, turning everything warm and golden as day fell to night. Lottie caught sight of her uncle near the Tickles' hive. The resilient little feather-footed creatures swarmed, picking up sticky bits in their mouths and piecing their home back together.

Lottie joined him, followed by Clement. Warwick pulled Hale's watch out of his pocket, then held it in the palm of his stone-gray hand. "A part of me knew who Hale was, deep down, I think. But she had clamped down on my heart and put it in a cage. I was desperate. I wanted to believe she was an angel sent to help."

Clement wrapped his arm around his father.

Warwick turned and peered in the direction of Ever After, then to the crumbled estate, and then in the direction of Vivelle. Finally, he sighed. "Oh, how very far we've wandered from home."

"But we still have time," Lottie said. "We're still on this side of the Veil."

"Yes," Clement added. "We're still alive."

Lottie had once thought that she was a girl only *half* alive, and that meant she somehow belonged in the Land of the Dead more than the Land of the Living. But, much like how the key to the enchanted garden played with the meaning of words, the key to making sense of everything that happened here did, too. She was alive, no matter how much she felt it or didn't feel it at any particular moment, half or mostly or barely at all. And what was more, she still had the chance to live a good and beautiful life.

"Absolutely," her uncle agreed. "We won't get back there in a day, that's for certain. It's been so long since I've stopped for rest. I'll need my faculties at the ready. Sorting it all out will take some effort on my part, and yours, too, Lottie, if you'll help me. Together, I think we can reverse the source of fuel. We'll have a new resource in abundance now, and I'm certain it can bring us back where we belong."

Lottie wasn't completely restored, and she didn't know that she ever would be. The things that had happened to her would, in many ways, leave her forever changed. But the magic in her surged at her uncle's words, starting in her chest, then finding its way to her fingers. They itched to paint again already—all the colors she had seen, and all the colors that were to come. The colors of the garden, and the people she loved, and the whole entire world. She itched to return to Vivelle and tell her story, the very true story of a girl who turned Living Gray and was finding a way through it.

"What fuel will you use now?" Clement asked.

The cardinal alighted, then perched on his shoulder.

Warwick knelt to the earth. He pressed his palm to it, letting the pulse of life that Lottie felt on her first peek into the garden pulse through him as well. He closed his eyes.

The moment the color seeped out of Lottie's world, she never would have believed something good could come from it. But somehow, it had. And it still would, too, in ways she hadn't even begun to imagine. She felt it in her bones. This was only the start.

Lottie thought of the clogged vat at the top of the tower, how the color had stopped the sorrow from surging. Magic was made of all the things a color could hold, all the things she held inside her heart. And it was tied together with something else in the most beautiful, powerful of knots.

"Hope," Lottie said. And then, she saw it. Just a prick, barely a sliver, but enough to know for certain. Her uncle's magic was the color of copper. And it still glowed.

"That's right." Warwick opened his eyes. "We'll get there on hope." He smiled up at his niece as the flicker of magic, thin as a wisp, danced inside his chest.

RESTORED

Lottie's room had also undergone its own great change since the day Forsaken nearly fell.

More light shone through the glass, setting a bright and cheery tone each morning. Her comforter shifted to a sky blue. The characters on the tapestries were now freed from their own sorrowful stories and had arranged themselves in a pleasant scene at a park, with kites flying and balloons floating in pastel pinks and yellows and blues. Their own uncertain futures looked much brighter now, just like hers.

"Lottie!" Clement's impatient voice ricocheted down the hall.

Lottie slipped on her shoes and snagged her satchel. She took a quick peek in the mirror, then gave herself a single spritz of her mother's perfume.

Warwick had taken her to visit the perfumery that her mother had bought it from, so Lottie could easily replenish her supply as needed. She felt a little more grown-up and a bit closer to her mother each time she wore the vanilla-gardenia scent.

"Coming!" Lottie shouted back. She ripped down the stairs and to the front door. It still opened without anyone pulling the handle, but this time it opened up to a bright, sunlit morning instead of a dull gray sky.

Forsaken had not only survived its stay in the In Between, but had now settled itself back in its original place at the edge of the oldest neighborhood in the city, where large estates towered over wide lots, only minutes from the heart of Vivelle.

Clement tapped his shoe against the pavement and the two took off at a run for the gate. The twin angels along either side looked down on them with smiles as they spilled onto the busy sidewalk.

"My dad's picking me up from my lesson, then we're going to Felicity's after, if you want to come," Clement said. "And we still need to pack for our trip."

Tomorrow, they were taking their first vacation as a family. Lottie couldn't wait to show Clement Vivelle's vast sea spread wide in all directions, dotted with sailing ships and their bright red sails. She couldn't wait to wiggle her toes in sand as fine and white as bleached sugar and let turquoise waves lap at her ankles once again.

"I'll be at the mural all morning." Lottie skipped while Clement picked up a jog. "I've got to get to a good stopping point before we go. But I could use a snack, if you want to drop a cookie off when you're done?" Felicity's Enchanted Treats had just rolled out their blooming teas and sugar cookies for spring. This year, they were cut into the shape of bright-colored garden-themed things like daisies, and butterflies, and tulips. Her mouth watered at the thought.

Clement agreed, then tagged her before taking off at a full-on sprint. They chased each other toward downtown, slipping around and through the crowds of Living Gray and a smattering of people still with their color. People who had no idea what the two children zipping past them had been through and how they'd come out the other side.

But Lottie aimed to change that.

Word of Henry Warwick's return had caused quite the stir. Someone as renowned as he was, who had splintered, then went where he did and was presumed dead but had survived it and returned to Vivelle somehow unsplintered wasn't an easy thing to ignore.

Turned out, people didn't really know what to do with a person who didn't fit the things they had always believed about the way things were, or what could be true.

They approached the tall, white columns of the

Great Magician Stage, where Clement had been taking lessons, following in his mother's literal footsteps.

"See ya, Lottie. I'll bring you a cookie." Clement jumped and clicked his heels off to one side before bounding up the stairs and heading in. His grass-green magic did a little leap of its own before he disappeared.

Lottie stared up at the impressive structure. So many things in Vivelle were named after the Great Magician, or referred to it in some way. But every attempt at something grand enough, or beautiful enough, or big enough to do the name justice fell so short compared to the things she had seen.

She pivoted, then headed toward the streets that would always be the most familiar to her, the ones that formed the building blocks of her first memories as a child. Where she learned to safely cross the road. The yard of the neighbor who placed shiny, colored stones in his potted plants just for Lottie to find. The building she used to live in, both a year and a half and a lifetime ago.

She paused and sat down at the bench across the street, then watched the windows of her old apartment. It didn't look like anyone was home, but someone else definitely lived there now. A different lamp rested on a different table by the window here. A different curtain hung from each side of a window there.

Lottie imagined her father, picking her up as a small girl and holding her, pointing out the new buds on the tree just outside. Her mother, twirling with her in front of the wide panes to an upbeat song. Lottie herself, smudging the glass with grimy fingers and Nellie coming along behind her, huffing in annoyance as she wiped the smudges away.

The memories played on for a moment each, a snapshot in time come back to life, before they all faded. Lottie reached up and gripped her locket tightly. She would keep those memories and so many more in her mind and in her heart forever.

She took a deep breath, then stood and continued on, down the block and around the corner. She stopped at the government building she had paused in front of on the day Nellie took her to meet Mrs. Hale. The wall she had imagined stepping through and blending into, where no one would know she had disappeared.

But she was now a once–Living Gray girl coming back into color who didn't blend in, no matter where she went. And this old gray wall wouldn't blend in for much longer either.

Another side effect of her uncle's return to Vivelle was the fact that he had left many friends behind who were thrilled to see him return. And, with her uncle's help, through one of those friends, Lottie had received her first commission as an artist.

She was already off to a good start. The left of the wall remained in gray tones and told the story of a girl and boy who found a burned garden covered in ice. As the mural moved on, she would paint the story of the garden's healing, as well as their own. With her gift, the painting would shift and the leaves would rustle, and the painted people would move inside it. It would tell a story that was also true, of two children who came back to life from the Living Gray.

Her sorrow had already made flowers grow and brought her new family together. And hopefully, her sorrow and her story would find a way to touch someone's heart who passed by here. Maybe someone who had faded would pause, and watch the story unfold, and would dream something different for their future, too.

She set down her satchel and got to work outlining the next section, pressing a white piece of chalk between two half-gray fingers. Before she knew it, the sun had risen nearly straight above her head, and Clement tapped on her shoulder, holding a cookie in his hand.

Her uncle stood behind him with a clear cup of tea that held a bright flower unfurling in the steaming hot water.

"It looks wonderful, Lottie. They'd be so proud." Warwick smiled as he handed her the cup.

THAT EVENING, LOTTIE'S SUITCASE RESTED BY THE DOOR TO her room, nearly packed and ready to go. She climbed into her bed and wrapped herself in her father's jacket, like always. His scent had faded, but she liked to lull herself to sleep by rubbing her fingers along the silly leather patches at its elbows until her mind gave in to sleep.

That night, Lottie dreamed of her parents, just like she'd hoped she would.

In her dream, four cardinals perched on the lowest branch of the healing tree. One for Dalia, one for Timmy, and one for her mother and father. They flew up into the air and fluttered above her head, chirping and singing. The garden swept her up in a warm, sweet wind. Her heart leapt with such a vigor that she felt like she might join them, lifting off the earth and setting for the sky.

It had been such a potent dream, the kind with the power to stick close long into the day. So when Lottie woke up the next morning, she wasn't surprised to find that the lightness still lingered in her chest, and that she thought she could still hear the cardinals' song.

She tipped her head, shaking away the fog of sleep.

No. It wasn't an echo of the dream somehow crossing

the veil between sleeping and awake. She could really *still* hear the birds singing. And it was coming from outside.

Lottie ran to the window, then yanked back the shades.

There they were.

Four red cardinals circled her window, singing and chirping, twirling around one another.

Lottie opened the panes and the birds glided into her room, spinning and swooping, creating a cyclone of bright color above her head.

She reached out her hands toward them. Two of the cardinals perched on her bedposts, and the other two landed on her outstretched fingers. She pulled those two in and brought them close to her cheeks. They bent their heads, and pressed their feathers against her skin.

"Thank you," Lottie whispered. This was the closest she'd felt to her parents since the night they died. Part of her wanted to keep the cardinals here forever, just to hold on to the feeling for as long as she possibly could. But the cardinals weren't meant to be a substitute for the ones she had lost, and they weren't meant to be kept or caged. They were meant to be a sign.

A clank sounded down the hall, letting her know it was almost time for breakfast, and their trip to the sea.

Lottie took a deep breath and then she released the

cardinals back out into the day. The group of them stuck close and danced in the sky a moment longer. Then they set off together, straight as an arrow, side by side back toward the peaks of Ever After, their wings reflecting the light of the morning sun.

At that exact moment, all the colors that love and magic and hope could hold shot out from Lottie's heart. They flooded her soul. They rushed her senses.

And they filled her to the brim.

ACKNOWLEDGMENTS

To my husband, John Paul, thank you for breathing life into this dream and for your continued unwavering belief in me. You are the banks to my river.

To my children, Felicity, August, Mary, and Zelie. Yours are the faces I see when I write, the hearts I think of as I decide what kinds of stories I want to tell. You are such a gift in my life, and your love, laughter, perspective, and perseverance inspire me each and every day. I love you so much.

A special thanks to Felicity for coming up with some of the whimsical, magical components of the Enchanted Garden, including the dragon daisies and Tickles. Your imagination helped bring the garden to life.

To Chloe Seager and the team at Madeleine Milburn, I'm so grateful for your enthusiastic support of me as an author, and for finding this book a wonderful home. Thank you for advocating for me, for finding *The Circus of Stolen Dreams* a home in two additional countries, and for being there for me whenever I need advice or have questions.

To Liza Kaplan, your spot-on editorial insights paved the way for me to figure out what this story needed to become. Thank you for seeing what I was trying to do and helping me to bring it out and translate it to the page. I'm so very proud of what we've done together, and it's been an honor to work with you on these stories.

To Talia Benamy, Krista Ahlberg, Abigail Powers, Marinda Valenti, Theresa Evangelista, Gaby Corzo, and Monique Sterling, I'm so thankful to have this team behind me as we send another book out into the world.

To Tracy J. Lee, thank you for the stunning cover; it is the most perfect way to wrap the words inside it.

To my family, Gary and Carrie Wondrash, Linda and Tom Steber, Kyle Wondrash and Marta Knodle, and the Savaryn family, thanks for enthusiasm and support all along the way.

To Catherine Bakewell, Rachel Greenlaw, Lacee Little, and Cyla Panin, thank you for being early readers of this story and for your feedback. I hope you are proud of how much it's grown since its earliest iteration.

To Alysa Wishingrad, your wisdom helped give me the courage to do the brave thing in order to get this story right. Every single moment of fear and uncertainty was worth it, just like you said.

To Juliana Brandt, Alyssa Colman, Jessica Olson, Summer Short, and Mindy Thompson, I'm thankful to have writerly friends, and your support has meant the world to me.

To Elizabeth May and Jennifer Mattern, I couldn't